Stephanie Doench

Black Heart Mississippi
Novel

Production and publishing house: BoD - Books on Demand, Norderstedt

ISBN: 9783753497570

Note: This work is also available in German. Under the title: "Ich fand mein Herz durch dich".

Herstellung und Verlag: BoD – Books on Demand, Norderstedt

ISBN: 9783753497570

Content:

"All people are different on the outside. But inside we are all the same. Each of us carries a heart that beats within. And a soul that carries it."

Stephanie Doench

The Prologue

Today in Mississippi, USA

It's a rainy day, the sky is dark, as if it should be. For when she left, the sky began to cry. Every single tear is for you, my love.

"In the darkness of grief, the stars of remembrance shine for those among us who miss you sorely. May God give you your final rest. The Lord keep you and protect you, so that you may now find rest and peace in eternity. The angels receive you. Patiently you wait for those you love. Lord give them all a long life and when they are ready for eternal death, you receive them with open arms, just as they once received you with open arms in your life," speaks the pastor.

Many people have come to the funeral. It is nice to see how popular she was. But there is deep sadness in me. Happy to have known her and yet sad to have lost her. The people present today and here are all dressed in black. They are all there, everyone wants to pay their last respects to her. I am sad, yes I am. Mum holds me in her arms, she is sad too. With her I can still understand it the most. But I, I have to say that I loved her infinitely.

She had not only class, but also style, dignity, grace and timeless elegance. If I had just a little bit of her, that would last me the rest of my life. But the bottom line is that I can say to her: what luck that I was allowed to meet you.

At first it is quiet and oppressive in her house. But then I look into the faces of the people, and more and more I recognize the radiance in their eyes. The radiance of happiness, to have known her and to have been a part of her life. I, too, belong to them. And Mum, Dad, Benjamin, his parents and all the others who have also taken them into their hearts. Black and white people, all united. Old and young, all talking to each other. They talk about the life they have lived and about the divinity of life in general. The happiness to be alive, to experience health, to have bread on the table and to be able to know your loved ones is a great gift. All of a sudden there is laughter and gossiping with God. Lord, in heaven, forgive us for this. We are all sitting together in fellowship. It makes me proud to kind of belong. They start clapping their hands, praising the Lord and singing with their powerful voices. I get goose bumps. Dad nudges me. He wants to encourage me to sing along. "Sing as loud as you can. Sing for her, sing for God and for heaven. Do it for her, she'd love it!" Even Benji claps and sings with the group. Shyly, I sit there not knowing if I can open up that much. I'm in mourning, as are all the other people, and yet they find the courage and sing a glorious praise. Then

Mum looks at me, she says nothing, but I know it's time for me now. Time to let go and give myself to life like she did. So I gather all my courage and clap my hands first. The other mourners become more and more euphoric; they clap their hands wildly and loudly, they dance and they celebrate life. It seems to me that they are celebrating their accomplished life. I join in at the word hallelujah. I continue, nothing, stops me, I sing with unity, I am not alone, I belong. I drop my reservations and just join in. In the end, I sing like there's no tomorrow. And by God, I enjoy it. What's most awesome for me is that I'm not worrying about being on my best behavior, I'm just living in the moment. I thank you in heaven for that. The singing seems to me to have brought some among the guests to ecstasy. But that doesn't matter, it is a togetherness that I didn't know in such a pronounced way a few years ago.

There was togetherness between me and my parents, also between me and Katy. But not with as many other people as are here today at her funeral service. And if I did know the feeling, then I suppressed it. It was only because of her that I was able to openly live out that feeling again. I thank her for that. After "Hallelujah" and "Price the Lord" were sung to the end, we fell together on the buffet. Because every celebration, no matter how sad, needs something decent to eat. Sweet potato casserole, corn, homemade bread and other delicacies are available for consumption. Now I sit there with my full plate and want to eat, but I can not. I can't get a bite down. "Take something to eat. You'll starve otherwise. She wouldn't have wanted you to go on hunger strike," Mum says to me. "I can't right now, I can't stop thinking about her." I feel sick, maybe I like talking more than eating. Benjamin and my dad are sitting next to me and I think they want to tell me to eat something. But they don't say it. They just know me way too well and know what a stubborn person is sitting next to them. I am glad when one of my grandmother's neighbors starts talking. I like to listen to people, it's distracting. 'I don't need to eat and maybe I'll learn more about her this way?", I wonder. The neighbor seems totally nice, she speaks in a calm manner, which in turn puts me at ease. "I didn't know she had a daughter and a granddaughter? I thought she was married to her novels," the neighbor elaborates and everyone has to laugh because before we entered her life, this was the case.

Apparently people know her well, it shows that she was a great person and was seen by her peers. I don't know what to say in response to the neighbor? I want to say so much and yet I can't. And at that moment I thank my mum, because she can answer unlike me, "We just met her recently." The man from the neighbor seems interested and wants to know more about us and the situation with my grandmother: "Why did you meet her so late?", my parents and I look at each other silently. We want to answer, because we are happy and proud about our almost unimaginable joining. The neighbor and his wife assure us that they don't want to offend us.

"It's totally okay that you ask," all eyes are on me. Because I'm the one who uttered those words. But I feel like I need to speak this. "The question is not why did we just meet her recently? But the question is mainly how we met her?" Everyone around me is silent, visibly puzzled by my way of responding to the question, because it begs an answer. Other neighbors, charity colleagues, and friends have gathered around the couch and are aiming their gazes specifically at my mouth. "Yeah right. Why and how did you meet her?" the outgoing and joyful neighbor wants to know. The other neighbors nod and agree wanting to know about it. Only Mum looks at me questioningly, "You don't have to say anything about it if you don't want to. No one is forcing you!" I realize that I have aroused people's curiosity with this, and what you start, you should finish. That's what I learned from their story. Finish what you start. So I look at my mum with a serious expression, sure that there's nothing I want more than to tell our story together. "It's okay. Please let me. It's important to me to tell the others!" My dad puts his hand on my back, this makes me feel like his strength is going over in me. My mom looks at my dad and then at me. "Okay honey. If you want to talk, talk." People stare at me, but in truth they are all looking at her, because it is her story and mine. The house mourners gather around us. Once I take a deep breath, I look into Benjamin's eyes; he winks at me and whispers softly, "You're doing this right, and I trust you." Briefly, I glance over at Grandma her black and white photo once more and thus begin to tell our story in front of everyone. I make them witnesses to our unbelievable yet true story.

This is my wish and I am sure also that of my unique and beloved grandmother.

"Well, that was so ..."

1.

Two and a half years earlier in Louisiana, USA

After countless years of pain, uncertainty and also fear, I was back in the hospital. It seemed to me that I had two lives. A life at home and a life in the hospital. Which one I liked better seems clear to anyone who has spent any length of time in the hospital. Sometimes it seemed to me that most of my life took place in the hospital. I read books, especially novels; they were about love and I would have liked more of that. Because my boyfriend Jack, (I don't even remember why I was still with him in the first place?) who I had known since school, was more of a burden than a joy to me lately. My name is Isabella, I am 20 years old and I suffered from a chronic heart muscle inflammation for several years. As a result, I was often weak and tired, and didn't always have the power I wanted to have. Because of the disease I had to spend more years than I could count in hospitals and special clinics. I was young and wanted to live my life, play sports, go to concerts, hang out with friends, study, and more. But I couldn't do most of that because my heart wouldn't take the effort. At least not always and to the fullest extent. My parents loved me, I had many friends who always visited me too and my boyfriend Jack, he was always there too, although I felt he would rather play sports with his boys and just enjoy his time. Even though I was sick and it was getting worse over the years and I was actually dealing with it enough, I felt for a long time that I was missing something and that something was wrong. It was like there was a part of me missing, something or someone that belonged to me that I was missing. And I felt that this feeling would not stop until I found what I was looking for. My parents and the doctors said it was part of my disease. The chronic heart muscle inflammation and being in the hospital all the time made me think too much. They all didn't take me seriously with my thoughts and feelings. I felt that there was still someone out there in the world who belonged to me and whom I missed. No one understood that in an empathetic way. I already felt like a crazy person. The other day, the doctors said to my mother, "You have always respected my cheerfulness, my wit and my way of dealing with the difficult situation. I was always a sign of steadfastness to them. But they had slowly come to suspect that I might be carrying a mild depressive disorder. My dad also asked me where his power girl had gone?

But what they all didn't realize was that I was still me, that I was still strong despite my illness. And yet I had such a strong connection to my heart that it was telling me not to give up and never to give up. Moreover, my heart was telling me: what you feel is right. Listen to me, because I'm still alive and I want to show you something.

What exactly my heart wanted to show me, I did not know at that time. But my inner voice told me, even if they thought I had gone crazy, that I should not stop hoping that one day my heart would find what it was looking for. And until then, they could all think of me what they wanted. My body was so weakened by now that I was unable to exercise at home, let alone walk up the stairs in our house, without feeling pure exertion. In fact, it was so bad that I had just reached the final stage of my illness. Hardly anyone got a new heart implanted. But since everything always had to be dramatic with me, it seemed clear that I would not be able to get by in this life without a donor heart. This thought frightened me. Because it was connected with hope. Would I really need a heart transplant and if so, would there be a suitable donor heart for me? Question after question crowded into my mind and seemed to unsettle the smart, confident girl from Louisiana. My dream of going to college was on hold at that moment. My illness, the fears that came with it, and the feeling of missing someone were my reality at that point. Another fact, my friends and family, they didn't understand me. Did I understand myself? I didn't really know. My blood work clearly indicated the battle my body was fighting with my heart. A battle I didn't want to fight. I didn't want to fight this battle. So many times I had asked myself, why was this happening to me? Why me of all people? So far, I had not found the answer. Although my friends kept saying that they admired my ambition and positive nature. But what good did that do me? My room at the hospital was filled with flowers, photos and other gifts. Jack brought me a stuffed animal the other day. It was supposed to cheer me up when I thought I was missing someone again. And such a thing should be my friend? I thought that he would stand by me and take my feelings seriously. A quiet feeling inside me said: Jack is nice, but his heart doesn't beat in the same language as my heart. Where our common path should lead us, I could not yet say from that time's point of view. Because unfortunately, I didn't even know for sure if I would even be alive next year? Sad, but true.

I would like to quench my thirst for knowledge and know what the future had in store for me? Whether Jack and I would stay together, whether I would ever get well, study, and most importantly, whether I would ever find what my heart was trying to find?

2.

At the same time somewhere in Mississippi, USA

A white house, the typical white columns on the porch adorned the entrance. In front of the house is a colorful sea of flowers. The flowers were so powerful that they almost covered the beauty of the house. The radiance of the flowers led the way to the entrance of the sophisticated house. Mixed with the scent of homemade lemonade and freshly cooked food, the house invited one to step inside. Overwhelmed by the delicious smells, one was almost compelled to stop in to see if the lovely smell was reflected inside the house?

"Gee Ava, your how many novels is this now?", Mary could barely keep count herself as she carried the laundry into Ava's bedroom. "The 51st," said the voice from the writing room. "I've never seen you take so long to finish a novel!", Mary wondered for quite some time. The woman from the writing room gave no information about her 51st novel. Ava was inhibited; something didn't seem right to her. "If you keep this up, even I'll be faster at writing than you," Mary laughed at not being able to finish Ava's novel. "You usually write as fast as lightning, but this time I don't recognize you, you're not getting old are you?", Mary couldn't contain herself from laughing. Taking a side swipe at her longtime friend was a pep talk for her, which should have a positive effect on Ava and her writing. Proud and head held high, Ava sat there trying to finish her novel. She felt it was time to make this novel different from the 50 before it. But she couldn't, she was affected, inhibited and afraid to reveal herself like that. Because every novel that was about love revealed a bit of her own story. A woman who loved life and also once loved a man. If she really managed to complete the fifty-first novel, and not in the same way she always did before, it would be her life-revelation. Would she actually be able to write it? "But not before playing a game of Scrabble," was part of the two women's nightly ritual. Most of the time, Ava won at the words game, but not this evening. Mary won handily. "I can't believe it. You weren't concentrating at all. Did you let me win on purpose?" laughed and grumbled Mary from Mississippi. 'What the heck is going on with Ava today?' Ever since she wrote her last novel, she's been unrecognizable,' Mary thought skeptically. "We're getting old. See you tomorrow Ava," Mary took in her friend's failure due to her advanced age. At the dressing room, Mary picked up her purse and left for the evening until she stepped back into Ava's house the next morning.

The next day was ushered in by the lovely warm sun. Ava sat piecemeal in her study, as she did every day, trying to finish her current novel. A warm cup of tea was to accompany her. Ava had never lost heart in her life, but since she was trying to catch up on her life a bit with this novel, she was getting slightly nervous. The old lady did not like this condition at all. Her romance novels were famous all over America and were highly prized by women worldwide. Why shouldn't she stay true to her lifelong rituals? She could have it easy and carry on as she had done with all her other novels before. So slowly, as the days drew to a close, she wondered, in her 80s, if it wouldn't make sense in her final days to try something completely different? She realized she had unfinished business in her life and didn't want to leave until that score was settled. While Mary was cleaning the windows in Ava's house, she stared surreptitiously at Ava's notes. "Do you still not have the bright idea, or what is missing from this novel?" her good friend Mary liked to know. Ava was silent at first, feeling caught by Mary, because no one knew her as long and as well as she did. Since Mary knew everything about her friend, she already suspected that something was not quite right this time. She was worried and thought that something was wrong with her health. Mary was half the age of her closest confidante. She was aware that at such an old age one doesn't have too many bright ideas anymore. But Mary had never seen such an intelligent woman as Ava before in her life. Until now, Ava always seemed to be in top shape; mentally as well as physically. The steady change since her friend wrote this novel and unfortunately didn't get to finish it, worried Mary greatly. However, she did not let the serious worries show. Two weeks later, her work was still unfinished. While Mary was doing the laundry, she noticed how thoughtful her friend seemed. "What do you say you and I go for a walk together again sometime?" Mary figured the exercise in the fresh air should inspire her friend to write. Ava had always been the health-conscious type and had never let herself go, even as she got older. That's when she had to coax Mary into any exercise that was outside of housework. Now it was the other way around, this time Mary was trying to talk her into coming out. But Ava seemed driven, as if she had to find the solution and finish what needed to be finished. Benjamin, whom everyone just called Benji, came over to Ava and Mary in a good mood. "Hello Ava, hello Aunt Mary," he greeted the two ladies. They greeted him back affectionately as well. Mary's nephew often visited Ava. He had the same happy, sunny disposition as his aunt. And the big mouth, too. The smell of freshly baked cookies often drew Benjamin there. Secretly, he would take a few more cookies because he could hardly resist. With his mouth full, he visited Ava in her office. "Maybe you'll give her a leg up so she can finish that novel. She's been working on it for half an eternity," Mary encouraged her nephew to ask. Benjamin was very fond of his aunt and also of the woman she worked for. The novels of his aunt's confidante were familiar even to her young nephew. For him, a different time seemed to apply in Ava's house, where writing and education still played a major role. There, the world was different from the world outside, which was largely dominated by violence and racism. Secretly, he had not only eaten the cookies, but also often read through the contents of Ava's romance novels. This, of course, he had never let get through to his buddies. He and Aunt Mary lived in a different world than Ava. The writer gave people a place in her house no matter where they came from, what color their skin was, or what their wealth was. Racism did not exist in this house. Ava never made a distinction between black and white. That day, without knowing it, Benjamin had put his foot in Ava's mouth. "May I join you?" Benjamin knew he was always allowed to sit next to the author, and today was no exception. He got right to the point. "Ava, your novels are always about love. And in the end, there's a happy ending between a man and a woman. But why are there never any children in your books and stories? Children are part of life. And when two people love each other, they want to have a child, don't they?" Benjamin asked with interest. This was too much for Ava. She immediately got up from her office chair, went to the window and looked out there. In a calm voice she said to Benji, "You should go now, your parents are probably waiting for you!" At that, she didn't even look at him, her gaze aimlessly directed out the window. The young man was irritated, because even though Ava could always appear very controlled and decisive, he had not expected this reaction. He had not expected that she would not answer his question. Completely stunned, he asked his Aunt Mary what was wrong with Ava at the moment? Concerned, she looked at her nephew and said the same thing as her boss, "You should go home now." Benji felt like he was in the wrong movie and both women were playing a trick on him. That was not unusual. Because in the past, the two women had often cooked up pranks, but they were usually uncovered at the latest as soon as Benjamin wanted to leave the house. But this time no one called after him: "Stop. Stop the car, it was a joke." No, Benjamin left the house not knowing what was going on with Ava and his aunt?

Weeks passed and the burden in Ava's mind and heart grew. Something from her past was trying to come to terms with, something she had always repressed and pushed away. But this time it was going to come up. Benjamin's question about why she only wrote about couples in her romance novels, but never about children, had upset her. Even more so than before. And that Benjamin made it clear that if two people love each other, then logically they would also want children, seemed self-evident to him. Ava reacted blocked. Inwardly as well as outwardly. She dismissed any questions from Mary. She closed herself off to her best friend and was even happy when she didn't ask about the current status of the new romance novel. At the moment, she just wanted to be left alone. "What, are you going to close yourself off and shut up for long? Are you sick, maybe? Is there anything I can do to help you? We've known each other for so long and know almost everything about each other. Why don't you tell me what I can do for you?" pleaded Mary to her closest confidante. Benjamin had not been back to her house for several weeks and since that day when he asked her the questions in the office. Normally that house was an open building to everyone. Joyfully and warmly everyone was welcomed by Ava and her housekeeper Mary. In matters of secrecy they served only a good purpose, the family around Mary did not need to hide. Her nephew, who secretly stole the cookies from the kitchen just because they were so delicious, so secretly Mary called Doctor Houston Junior to ask him to check on Ava. Shortly thereafter, Doctor Houston Junior appeared at Ava's house, still surrounded by colorful, fragrant flowers. Ava was visibly uncomfortable that the doctor had come all this way to see her. She looked slightly ashamed and said directly that she had nothing and that he had come for nothing. "I don't understand, doctor, who actually called you here?", she already had a suspicion. Her eyes fell on her best Mary, who felt caught and turned away. "So that's where the wind is blowing from," Ava added. But the doctor didn't miss the chance to examine Ava thoroughly. The lungs were listened to, blood pressure was measured, furthermore Doctor Houston junior asked Ava some questions. Last but not least, he drew her blood. Ava reacted sourly, because after all she had always been healthy, had done sports, worked steadily and kept fit. "Madame, you are no longer 20 years old and if I may take the liberty of saying, you are 80 years old and I therefore consider it my duty to draw your blood. Even if you think it unnecessary!" Doctor

Houston Junior said goodbye and went back to his office. Mary immediately went to the kitchen so that she would not have to give any account to her friend. This was to serve Ava right; she retired to her study. A week later, the results from Doctor Houston Junior's visit arrived. "I knew I was in perfect health. You could have saved yourself the trouble," Ava said smugly. But Mary wouldn't be a friend if she didn't have something to say about that: "And, still, you have something. You've been acting all weird for weeks and every question you're asked, you dodge or ignore. I'm just worried about you!" Ava felt guilty and knew it couldn't go on like this. Either she would write out what she should have written out years ago. Or she would be silent forever and accept her silence while she was still alive. 'After all, silence can be made more bearable with a glass of wine in the evening,' she thought to herself. 'But a decision must be made; better now than sometime. Because sometime may already be too late. At my age, one should not wait so long for decisions, but make them and implement them quickly,' she also thought to herself. "I'm too old to put off making decisions," the fine old lady motivated herself. It was not clear to her whether this would be her last novel? But the possibility would have had to be considered, so she mentally asked herself the question: 'Is this my last novel? And if so, can and will I reveal myself in it?' Before nightfall, Ava suggested to Mary that she not go home yet, but join her for a glass of wine or two. Mary gratefully accepted the offer and lit the romantic fireplace with a fire. Together and just as they did then, the two women sat by the fireplace while they talked about life and its pleasures. Accompanied by one glass of red wine after another and much laughter, the ladies left the entire bottle of red wine down to the last drop before saying goodbye to each other. Benjamin picked up his aunt in the car so she wouldn't have to drive home alone and slightly tipsy from the alcoholic beverage. "You know you can always sleep here with me, too," Ava implored Mary. But even though the relationship between the two women was so good, she slept at her house anytime.

That night Ava slept soundly, intending to wake up tomorrow having found a solution to finishing her novel.

3.

Back in Louisiana, USA

In the meantime, Isabella had returned home after her hospital stay. Extremely weakened and tired from her chronic heart muscle inflammation, she had to continue resting at home. The slightest exertion would have resulted in a relapse back to the hospital. Any movement that would have gone toward exercise was forbidden to her. She was 20 years old and wanted to live. To have fun and do what her friends of the same age did. Her parents always wanted to protect her and had almost overprotected her out of love. This annoyed Isabella at times, but she was aware of how nice it was to have family and friends by her side. Her sunny nature brought much light and warmth into the hearts of those around her. Despite her illness, she had never let it take away her zest for life and was always up for a joke. But the last hospital stays had taken their toll on her. Far too often she was away from home and had to spend more and more time in the hospital. The doctors and nurses were constantly taking care of Isabella and the other patients. And still, the last stays in the clinics were hardly bearable for Isabella. Even her parents had noticed that she had lost some of her positive nature, which made them sad and thoughtful. They loved their daughter more than anything and wanted only one thing: for Isabella to stay alive!

Further and further Isabella struggled with her illness, the thoughts about her future and this strange feeling, which visited her more and more often lately. The feeling was like a kind of compass, a sense that wanted to tell her to set out to search. But who or what was there to look for? Something was missing in her life, she was missing someone and further Isabella asked herself in her mind as she sat on her bed at home, 'Or do I mean missing someone because in truth I am missing myself?'

Because I miss my life that I would like to live but can't? Or because I miss having fun with my friends and going out, playing sports and studying?' Isabella stumbled and became sad. Continuing to think, what was that strange feeling in her heart trying to tell her? The following night, Isa couldn't sleep. She tossed and turned in her bed. Beads of sweat ran down her forehead, her pajamas were soaked with sweat. Her parents next door noticed that their daughter wasn't feeling well and came to her immediately. "Honey, what's wrong? Can't you sleep? Should we call the doctor?" her mother asked excitedly. "Gee mum, can't you leave me alone for once?", Isabella turned away. Sometimes she felt like she was suffocating from her mother's care. Now Isabella's father intervened, "Isa, you're sweating wet, Mum will help you change and I'll get you a wet rag for your forehead." Her father's calm manner did her good. She knew her mother worried too, but she dramatized more. Her dad, on the other hand, seemed level-headed, especially in his voice. Often, with a grin on her face, Isabella thought to herself that her dad could have worked as a hypnotist instead of a police officer. His soothing voice lulled her to sleep as a child. But it just so happened that her dad, through his job as a police officer, knew how to defuse difficult situations. After Isabella changed and the wet rag lingered on her forehead, she lay with her mother in her arms. Quietly, a thank you passed her lips, and her mother stroked her hair while Isabella fell asleep.

The next morning, she realized that perhaps one reason her heart was missing someone might be the relationship between her and Jack? Isabella often had the premonition (or, one could say, the energetic opinion) that she didn't want to keep doing this to Jack. She didn't know if she could put him through the situation? Most of the time she was in the hospital and when she was home, she was weakened and couldn't do anything that other 20-year-olds were doing at the same time. She kept telling herself that it would be best for them if only one of them was burdened. It was enough if she was sick and had to live with it. She didn't want to burden her old school friend Jack with this. Besides, he no longer spoke the same language she did. Jack no longer understood her with her feelings. Thinking the other way around and positively, he still seemed to like Isabella a lot. He visited her regularly, brought her gifts, and had never talked about possibly ending the relationship.

So what was she to do? Isabella decided not to do anything yet in this case and let time drag on.

"Katy is coming today, right? You're happy she's coming, aren't you? And to celebrate that you're back home and because Katy is coming, I'm about to bake an apple pie," Isabella's mother's joy was evident on her face. Isa was happy too, because the visit of her best friend plus mom's much desired warm apple pie were double the trump card. Isabella thought to herself that she had been unfair to her mother lately, and that even though she had done so much for her. It was about time for some mother-daughter action together. And what could be more appropriate than baking the apple pie together? To surprise her mother, she joined her in the kitchen without any announcement and put on an apron. Annabelle's eyes widened when she saw her daughter standing in the kitchen wearing an apron. "Will you help me?" was barely uttered before Isa took her mother in her arms. Completely overwhelmed, Annabelle stood speechless and took her daughter in her arms as well. Afterwards, they baked together what was probably the best apple pie in all of Louisiana. Isa peeled the apples, cored them and cut them into small pieces while her mother prepared the dough. "This is what lunch smells like. These are my girls. Can I have a nibble?", Isabella's father came home in a good mood in his police officer uniform. "Dad, you have to go right back to work. We'll leave you a piece of the apple pie though," Isa said as her father looked at her with a long drawn out snout. "OK. Fine, we'll leave you two pieces," she grinned. "That's my daughter," Thomas said as he shoved a piece of apple into his mouth and went back out on duty. Together, mother and daughter finished baking the pie and cleaned up the kitchen. Swing and jazz music played in the background. The women were having fun and moving their feet to the beat of the music. A great noon passed until Isabella retired to her room to wait for her best friend Katy. Meanwhile, the apple pie was cooling down in the kitchen. She realized, as she spent time with her parents, that the feeling of missing someone had to be outside this family circle. But where then? What was her heart trying to say? Soon enough, she would find the answer.

In the afternoon, Katy finally appeared. Many letters, postcards, messages and gifts from all her friends she had brought for Isabella. One by one she read through the cards and opened the gifts. Of course, the girls posted the happily shot pictures for their friends on social media. Isabella opening the gifts, reading the letters, etc. Everything was documented by photo and uploaded, of course, so that the others were included. "Too bad you weren't at the volleyball tournament. You would have laughed your ass off when Jeremy and Mike banged their heads against each other. That was a bang, I'll tell you that. They were both hurting, but the crowd was laughing. Jeremy was even hurt so bad he had to go to the infirmary," reported her best friend from campus. The two had to laugh out loud at the image of the volleyball accident. The good humor continued continuously. Isa got back into her old form and threw her pillow at Katy. The pillow fight started simultaneously while Annabelle tried to enter her daughter's room without being hit by a pillow. "If you hit me, I'm afraid your apple pie will have to go, too. Or do you want to scrape it up from the floor?" It was quiet for a moment, and the girlfriends briefly ended their pillow fight. The smell of the cake made it quite clear what the young ladies' priorities were. "From pillow fight to cake fight. Well let's get to it," Isabella and Katy sat up straight and enjoyed the delicious, juicy apple pie. Isabella's mother retreated, leaving the girls to their realm. Between having fun, taking pictures, communicating with the other friends, and eating pie, Isabella thought about confiding in her best friend. Should she dare? After all, Katy had always stood by her and could understand her in any situation. But was this topic perhaps a bit too high and too abstract for young Katy, who was commuting between university, sports and her job? Isabella wasn't quite sure about this one, but of everyone she knew, she would be the most likely to confide in her. While Katy was chattering and chattering, Isa was already getting quite an earful from her friend. She told her about the campus, the class schedule, the boring professors, and the anything but boring boys at the university. It made Isabella feel like she belonged, as if she was just on vacation and would soon be going back to college. But the reality was different. Her chronic heart muscle inflammation had progressed so far by now that a normal everyday life remained a long way off. "My head is fully capable, only my body is not," was important to her to express, although everyone knew that. Isabella had become so mature and adult through her illness that she reflected and assessed herself well. But could she also realistically assess Katy's opinion? Or would she end up telling her, along the lines of, "Stop fooling around already! Don't take this feeling seriously. It's because you've been sick for so long. You're getting into something. It doesn't mean anything." Would she tell her like that? That's what Isabella was afraid of, because she didn't like to hear that. She wanted to be taken seriously, treated fully and fairly. And so she continued to listen to her friend gossip about university happenings. Sometimes she tried to catch her breath and catch the right moment. Whenever the right moment seemed to come, it was gone just as quickly. Katy was almost unstoppable when she talked, setting a pace that even the loquacious Isabella couldn't follow, let alone interrupt. So she tried to make an attempt in several attempts, but she did not succeed. Isa almost closed her eyes with fatigue after her crony had talked for an hour straight, giggling incessantly. 'I don't think I'll get another turn today,' she thought to herself. There was no end to the giggles and laughter between the two friends. Katy talked devotedly about her crush that she didn't notice, moving more and more to the edge of the bed and finally tumbling out of bed full blast. There was a crash. But the pain was not too great, because the two girls laughed so loudly that the fall from the bed was not so bad for Katy. Annabelle wanted to see if anything had happened to the two because she had heard a dull bang. Isabella enlightened her that her friend was so swarming, thereby overlooked the end of the bed and fell down from it. This was not a big surprise for her mother, because it was no secret that the two of them had always had great fun. She went back downstairs and could continue to hear the girls giggling from upstairs. After the fun time, Isabella was motivated to confide in Katy. How would she react? Loosely following the motto, don't think, do, Isa took a chance when her best friend took a breath. Silently, Isabella sat there and looked at Katy. "You want to tell me something? What is it? Don't you have long?", Katy had tears in her eyes, thinking that Isabella was going to tell her that her time was about up. Secretly she had been worried for a while, she had known Isabella since she was a little girl, she was her best friend and she didn't want to lose her. At least not at this point in time. That would be too early, to step out of life at the age of 20. To whom should she confide her stories from university, with whom should she gossip, laugh and cry? No, that would definitely be too soon and she hoped that Isabella would not tell her anything about dying.

Again, Isa gasped and told her friend that she actually had to report something to her. Katy knew Isabella so well that she knew to give her the space to talk now. So she sat down quietly and straight. She fixed her eyes on her unfortunately terminally ill friend, combined with the hope that she should live for a long time. By making eye contact, she wanted to make it clear to Isabella that she would now listen attentively, after all, that's what one did as a best friend. "I ... I ...", Isabella began to stutter and became nervous. This did not escape Katy's notice either. She didn't know how to get the beginning right? Finding the right words wasn't usually difficult for her, but today especially so. It's not as if she wanted to tell her a secret, some outrage she had committed, something horrible. No, it wasn't any of that. It was just about her feelings. Only why was she so afraid of her friend's reaction, why was she afraid to reveal herself? "You can tell me about it another time if you want. You don't have to now if you can't!", Katy in truth wanted to block the conversation because she feared the worst and she didn't like hearing that today. She wanted to remember her friend the way she did that day. With pillow fights, cake and men's stories. But definitely not hear that she would soon bury her friend.

Isabella didn't do her friend the favor of neither ending the conversation now nor dying. She grabbed her heart and began to tell.

"Now tell me, what's wrong?", Katy wouldn't let up. Isabella tried to find the perfect words in her head to describe her feeling. But no matter how perfect the words were, it couldn't begin to reflect how she was feeling. Katy sat there expectantly, eyes wide. "You know that feeling when everything changes inside you, but your environment stays the same? It's a weird feeling, and it's something you have to come to terms with." Katy wanted to know what Isabella meant exactly? "For some time now I've had a strange feeling inside me, right in my heart and I don't know where it comes from?" Katy was just about to crack up inside, because her fear that Isabella had a weird feeling inside her could indicate that her body was about to say goodbye to her. 'Oh no, I had a feeling. She's going to die, what did I do wrong in life that God would take my best friend?' Katy floated in thought as Isabella continued. "And, what bothers me the most is that no one takes me seriously, not the doctors, not my parents, not anyone. They all think I'm crazy. And do you know how stupid it feels when no one takes you seriously?" the terminally ill young woman fussed. 'Yes, I do, I take you seriously. In fact, I take you seriously enough to realize that your body is trying to tell you, 'Hey, you there. You're going to die soon. Get ready for it.' Katy's thoughts were moving more and more in the direction of Isabella dying soon. But she hadn't voiced any of those thoughts yet. 'Why doesn't she say anything? Does she think the same way as my parents and the doctors?' Isabella was worried, she wished for compassion and understanding. Still, she kept talking. "And, more importantly, my heart has felt for some time that it misses someone. So to be precise, I miss someone in my heart. But I don't know who?"

Katy's ears perked up and she didn't understand the world anymore. One minute Isa was talking about having a funny feeling, and now she was missing someone. "What do you mean? You're missing someone in your heart? Or your heart is missing someone?", Katy wished for an accurate and plausible explanation. "It's a very different feeling than before. I know I'm sick, but that now, it has nothing to do with the illness. I feel that. My heart wants to tell me something. And there is this feeling that someone is missing in my life, I have to look for them. I miss someone and I keep asking myself: who is it? And what does my heart want to tell me?", Isabella looked at her best friend questioningly. She had tears in her eyes and her face contorted bitterly. It was obvious that this was a serious matter for her. Katy took Isabella tightly in her arms and hugged her, Isa reciprocated. It felt good for her, she felt compassion from her friend. "Do you have any quiet idea who is missing in your life? Or who you might be missing?", Katy's questions gave Isabella hope. Finally, someone who was genuinely interested in her concerns. "No. I've been thinking for so long, what is my heart, and by extension my body, trying to tell me? Who I might be missing, who I'm missing, or a sign up above from heaven or from my surroundings? No. I just don't know. But my sense is so deep, it's inside me and it's not going away!" Katy, after all, seriously pondered whether the signs from Isabella's body were meant to mean that she was so sick and therefore had to die soon? Possibly her body was trying to warn her or prepare her for the fact that soon she would no longer be alive. This was a shock for Katy, who was otherwise also funny and full of life, and who didn't have much else on her mind besides studying and men. But she always kept an open ear for her oldest friend. "Maybe you misinterpret the feeling of missing. Your body is so sick and weakened, it just wants to tell you that: so that you should take care of yourself, your body and especially your heart. Probably it means only that and nothing else. You are sick and I hope it will not get worse. It may be that your heart is trying to tell you that," was Katy's opinion.

"No, no, no. It isn't. I know I'm terminally ill and I probably won't get old. But the feeling is something else. Please believe me. This time it's something new, a feeling that was never there before. My heart wants to tell me something. I miss someone," Isabella continued to fight the tears. Her heart ached, her pulse increased and her face contorted. Katy didn't think this was how this conversation and visit with her friend was going to end after cake and pillow fights. She didn't want to be superficial, so she tried to put herself into her friend's feelings. And to take them seriously. Katy began to think hard, while Isabella disappeared into the bathroom for a moment. And because Katy could think best while she was moving, she went downstairs to Annabelle and got two glasses of water upstairs. 'I don't believe it. 'I've got it. That might be an idea?' Katy accepted the glasses and the water from Isabella's mother. An idea struck her like lightning. She looked at Annabelle and immediately had a thought she wanted to share with Isabella. Upstairs, Isa was back in her room and the tears were wiped away. Her friend handed her a glass of water to drink. Gladly, Isabella accepted the fresh drink and sat back down on her bed. Katy did not dare to share her flash of inspiration with Isabella directly. This time Isabella would think of her that she was crazy. Usually Isa was known for her extraordinary ideas and funny suggestions. This time it bubbled out of Katy. "I just saw your mother," Katy said, staring at Isabella. "I know. You've seen her a million times," her friend replied, not sure what she was trying to tell her?

"When I saw your mother, it came up in me. It's an insane idea. You told me once that you knew your grandfather was dead. And your grandmother; she's supposed to be alive, but you never met her. So you don't know who she is, she should be old by now. Maybe and it's just a thought? Maybe you miss your grandma?" That was what Katy really needed to say. Would she lynch Isabella for that now? At least she didn't burst into tears, but she didn't laugh either. No reaction from her friend. "Isabella? Please say something. Isa?", Katy thought she had done great damage with this question and consideration. But Isabella; she sat there thinking. She was just thinking. Back and forth, introspective, powerful in thought. Moments passed and Isa was still thinking about what Katy had told her. Her friend noticed that Isabella was now retreating inside. Racked with reproach, Katy said goodbye to her best friend for the day, hoping that Isabella would not let the questioning bother her too much. Isa accompanied her friend downstairs to the door. A strong, firm, friendly hug goodbye supported both young women.

The heart patient became pensive. Was there any truth to her school friend's suspicions? Would it really be about her unknown grandmother? The subject had always preoccupied her, but it was never so important that her life depended on it. She had a choice now between going upstairs to her room or joining her mother and perhaps broaching this delicate subject? 'I'm going to count to ten. And when I get to ten, I'll make a decision. Go to my room or bring up the subject, even if Mum blocks again', Isabella told herself in her mind as she put her foot on the first step up. She hesitated and put her foot back. As if it was her intuition, she went to her mother Annabelle. She carried such fear within her, because until now her mother had never spoken much about the subject of her grandmother. Her mother was at peace with herself and happy with her family, work and life. She didn't want to hurt her mother or even hurt her. But grateful for her best friend's tip, she wanted to try again to approach her mother on the delicate subject of her grandmother. Outside, it was already starting to get dark. The day passed quickly and so far had a little bit of everything. From fun to thoughtfulness, everything was there. But what followed, no one in the family had expected ...

In the living room, Isabella then dared the unspoken. "Mum, I wanted to bring up another subject. To be exact ...", Isa faltered and interrupted her sentence. Annabelle looked questioningly at her daughter, who launched another attempt to finish the sentence. "Haven't you ever wondered who your birth mother is? And if she is still alive today?" Isabella was eager to hear her mother's reaction. She also promptly replied, "What should I say or answer you? It is what it is, and I have never let this unsettled question affect me negatively. You know that I have always accepted the situation as it is. I have accepted that I do not know who my mother is. Merely I know that my biological father is already deceased. He was a black man. And my mother is white. But that's all I know. Only this little information I have had all my life. And it's okay like that." Annabelle affirmed and protected herself that way. Isabella couldn't understand that, that it was just okay for her mother. For herself, nothing seemed okay right now. "Why do you think I got pregnant with you so late? I wanted to make it okay. Because even though I was adopted as a very young child and I was fine there, I still always had inhibitions about becoming a mother myself. I didn't want to have to give my child up for adoption. No, I didn't want that. The same mistake should not happen to me. I enjoyed studying and was proud of it, and then it came as it had to come. I met your father. He was the right one and with him I brought you into the world. For some, this late maternal happiness was unexpected, but for me it was a good thing. I was finally ready for it," Annabelle got off her chest. "That's all well and good that it turned out that way for you and that you're doing well with it. But what about my grandmother? With your mother? Don't you want to meet her? Maybe she's already dead, she should be old by now? I don't understand you. Why don't you want to know where you come from?" Isabella seemed energetic and talked herself into a rage. Her mother's face reddened slightly; the subject seemed inappropriate to her, because she was finished with it. "Your dad and I, we wanted to give you life and at the same time do something good at work. Your dad is out on the streets as a cop and I'm a social worker. I can do a lot of good with that. I help other people who need my help and I do a good job with it. You can see it. Especially the black people have it hard here. I know my dad was black too and I feel he would have liked my work."

"That's just it. You have a sense that you would please your late father with your work. And I have a sense, for quite some time now, that I'm missing someone in my heart. I sense that, I feel that, I live that. And I can't understand that you have a sense for your dead father, but your mother, who may still be alive, you don't care about that," Isabella grew louder. The argument between the two women threatened to escalate. The mother suspected something else: "Unfortunately, it's not my fault that you, my darling, are very ill and can't lead the life that was actually intended for you. I studied social pedagogy and I know that you would also like to make the university unsafe every day. But that's not possible, and I'm so sorry for you. You still have to make the best of it. God and we, your parents, will help you." With that, Annabelle had hit a painful spot in her daughter. "Mom, that's not the point. I'm missing someone I don't know about yet. And maybe that's my grandma I miss so painfully? How can you not want to know who your mother is and fight to meet her? All these years, why have you never tried to meet her?"

Isabella's father had just come home from his shift and couldn't believe his eyes or his ears. A fight between his two girls, he had never seen that before. He kissed his wife in greeting and asked directly what was going on? In any case, there was not much to see of harmony. "The same subject again. She asked about her grandma," Annabelle explained to her husband. He liked to answer his daughter: "We've explained that to you before. Your mother is done with the subject. She doesn't know who her biological mother is and whether she is still alive? But at some point, an unresolved issue must be closed internally. Otherwise you drive yourself crazy." Isabella understood the words, but could hardly comprehend the content. She would want to know. "It's not that I never tried to find out who she is. For years in the past I talked to the authorities. But never was there any informative information for me. I was told that everything went well with my adoption and that years later they have no information about my birth parents. Even my lawyer could not help me. As I said, all I know is that it was a mixed relationship. So that my mother is a white woman and my father was a dark-skinned man. And that my father has been dead for a very long time. And probably there's a high probability that I was born in another state and then taken away. So here to Louisiana. The papers about where I was born and the names of my parents supposedly no longer exist," the mother appeared strong and tried to keep her composure, but deep pain over the uncertainty also sat inside her. She bore her fate against all odds, yet with composure. The parents knew that there was not much they could do about the situation. They had tried together in the past to get any information about the origin of Annabelle. After many years of painful experiences and a long struggle, Isabella's mother had accepted her personal life story and decided to live happily ever after. With Thomas by her side, she had become a strong woman and mother to Isabella, a heart patient.

But for Isa, none of this was explanation enough. She didn't want to hurt her parents, but something inside her said her cause was so important that she didn't want to just sweep it under the rug. In high school, she had led various groups, led a protest, and if there was anything good to fight for, she was most likely to be there. From there, Isabella was used to standing up for an important cause and not giving up rashly. This time she had overstepped the mark as she had unwillingly overlooked her mother's feelings. "Mum I don't understand. How can you just let it go? Don't give up the fight! What if it's her I'm missing? She's with us after all and I feel I need her. Yes, I feel more and more that it's her," Isabella didn't stop pleading with her mother. Determined that her grandmother had to be found (hoping she was still alive), she pestered her parents. She didn't realize how painful the unresolved issue was for her mother.

The war of words went back and forth. It became louder, more uncomfortable and more intimate. Tempers were running high and there seemed to be no end to the discussion. Annabelle and Thomas had their own opinions, but Isabella didn't let up. Her mother had tears in her eyes, looked tense and strained. But Isabella herself looked as if she was on the verge of a breakdown. Then the situation escalated in the otherwise peaceful house. There was shouting and discussion; Isabella clung to the edge of the table. Her face and upper body were covered in sweat. The liquid beaded down from her face. She turned white as a sheet and just stared into space. "Oh, my God. No!" cried Annabelle as Isa sank into her mother's arms, unresponsive. "She's collapsing. I'm going to call an ambulance. Keep her conscious. I'll hurry," Thomas placed the emergency call. None of the people involved had wished for a situation like this or had any idea that the day would end with a complete escalation. The ambulance arrived quickly and drove the heart patient swiftly to the hospital. There, everything happened very quickly, because the doctors and nurses had known Isabella and her illness for years. While the young patient was being treated intensively, her parents blamed themselves. They supported each other, held each other in their arms and were stunned by the misfortune that had just occurred. The next night, the two did not leave her side. The attending doctors discussed whether they should put Isabella into an artificial coma? But they decided against it. The parents were fully aware of the seriousness of the situation and prayed that this had not been their daughter's last day. The quarrel should not be the reason that their beloved daughter had to pass away from them. "You did everything right," Thomas repeated forcefully to his wife, the usually strong social worker was at her wits' end. "I'm so glad I have you, thank you," Annabelle addressed her husband. "We're going to make it, it's going to be okay. I promise you," he added. Wearing mouth guards and protective suits, the parents sat in the intensive care unit holding their daughter's hand. Unfortunately, her parents' touches didn't do too much good. Her condition was worsening by the hour. Her blood counts were at the worst they had ever been. Suddenly, everything happened very quickly.

Hospital staff rushed to Isabella's side because her heart was no longer threatening to keep up. The parents suddenly had to leave the intensive care area and feared for the life of their still so young daughter. The head physician took them by the side and explained to them that Isabella's situation was serious. They would do everything, but they should not get their hopes up. Annabelle also collapsed and was caught at the last second by her husband. "No, thank you. I don't want any sedatives, a glass of water is enough for me," the strong woman pulled herself together and fought along for the life of her only daughter.

The next day, Isabella almost died in the hospital. The place where she had been so many times before because of her chronic heart muscle inflammation. Should this place have been her last? The hospital staff tried very hard and gave everything for the otherwise so joyful and life-affirming patient. But it was serious, the last hours of her seemed to be beating ...

The doctors agreed, their patient had reached the last stage of her illness and urgently needed a donor heart. The last way should be postponed for a long time or if possible, never come to fruition, but it had to be done. In the conference room, the attending physicians shared the information with the parents. "It is urgent," was all the parents had been able to perceive. Then the real work of the doctors and the professor of heart transplantation began. In their database, which consisted of millions of protected information, they searched as a team for a suitable donor heart for Isabella. A lot of things had to be taken into account, because a lot of the donor and recipient had to match. And that's where the big problems began. Nothing was impossible, but it was still difficult. Especially with this sensitive topic. Not only did the blood values have to match; organ donation also entailed risks. In advance, the doctors gave Isabella medication to suppress her own immune system. This was done to prevent rejection of the heart that was foreign to her body. The whole thing increased the risk of infection with bacteria or fungi, the family was told. But the path seemed inevitable. The parents knew that one in ten transplant recipients dies in the first year after the heart transplant. From there, the fear was great. But not getting a donor heart meant death soon enough. "It can't be that hard, why can't they find anything?" the worried father asked. He knew that the search for a donor organ could sometimes take a long time. And yet it didn't go fast enough for him; after all, his daughter's life was at stake. The family seemed desperate, because after a long search and research, the doctors could not find a suitable donor heart for their daughter. They continued to hope, pray and believe in a miracle. Isabella was by now completely weakened. Her heart, body and immune system just weren't doing what they were supposed to. But her spirit, head and thoughts were still working at 100 percent. While everyone around her was going crazy, scared and worrying, Isabella's thoughts were solely on her unknown grandmother. Her heart was in an exceptional situation. The feeling that her heart was missing someone was growing. The days in the hospital were long and the time seemed endless to her. All the more thoughts and questions drifted through her head. Isabella asked herself questions about her grandma: 'What does she look like? Who is she? What has she experienced and how has she lived? Who and what does she love?'

The next day was to be a retreat. Just like every hospital stay, this time her childhood friend Jack came to visit. Beforehand, Thomas told him what had happened at home and that his girlfriend was now waiting for a donor heart. Jack did not want to blame Isabella because she was in a critical condition. He himself was only allowed into the intensive care unit for a short time, and only with a mouth guard plus a protective suit. Not even the obligatory kiss on the forehead as a greeting was allowed. Nevertheless, her boyfriend could not resist a side blow and asked the critical question, whether this had to be? "What do you mean? Whether this should have been? You don't take me and my feelings seriously," Isabella added nothing more. Despite her poor condition, she could be upset, and she was tremendously so. Empathy she expected from Jack, but all that came was a sharp question that did not come from a positive basic attitude. She was not in a position to separate herself from Jack right now; she was just too physically unwell. She wished he would leave quickly, and he did. "I guess it's best if I go now," he lingered with her for a brief moment and then briskly disappeared through the door. Being clouded over Jack lasted only a short time. She was preoccupied with her illness, visiting her parents who didn't leave her side, and motivating thoughts of meeting her grandmother. Let this be her last wish. Her boyfriend had indicated through the flower that he did not support her in the search for her grandmother and he thought this was a gross nonsense. So Isabella made hopeful plans to go searching after her hospitalization and recovery, to do her heart justice.

For weeks Isabella struggled in the hospital, still no matching donor organ was found for her. The situation began to become critical. Doctors tried to keep Isabella alive, but time was running out. "She is about to jump, we need to find someone as soon as possible," the father heard that doctor say to the other. Everyone around Isabella felt powerless. Waiting and not knowing what would happen seemed to become a huge burden for everyone involved. On Sunday, Annabelle and Thomas were in church praying for their daughter with the other believers. The whole congregation was behind them, giving strength. Isabella was more preoccupied with plans to eventually find her missing grandmother than letting her state of illness drag her down. She had to live; for herself and for her dream of locating her grandmother. Her biggest worry was that she was no longer alive. And because Isabella still had hope, she kept going. Day after day, week after week, she did not give up. No, never! 'Please God, give me a donor heart and let me live. Let me live to meet my mother's mother at least once. That's all I ask of you. Amen,' Isabella spoke to herself. Her best friend Katy was also allowed to visit Isa and was ashamed to have voiced the idea that Isabella's heart might well be missing her grandmother. No one in the family held it against Katy. For far too long she had been a part of this family, where discussions were generally frequent.

4.

Back in Mississippi, USA

Things were lively again at Ava's house. Just like in the old days. Visitors came and went, there was a lot of talking, singing and laughing together. As is the way of life, neighbors and friends also told of unpleasant things and problems that burdened them. Also about strokes of fate. Ava had an open ear for everyone. Mary also often sat in, listened and always had a lot to say herself. None of the guests said it out loud, but the reason Ava's house was so popular was not only because of the charming hostess, but also because of her closest confidante, the housekeeper and best cook from all over Mississippi. "Mary, when are you going to make that delicious chicken and your famous mashed potatoes again?" a friend of the house asked. "Oh, what. I want fresh lemonade, plus the best crumble I've ever had," interjected old Mister MC Kenn. "You can't have everything," Mary winked at him. "Well, I'll be. Then I'll go again," the whole company laughed loudly. Benji, Mary's nephew, was also there again, as he was almost every day. "Benjamin, go out and hang with the guys. You can't be visiting with us two old ladies every day. I love you, my nephew, but I don't understand," Mary was puzzled. The ideal and funny world around Ava's house attracted not only middle-aged people and seniors, but also young people. Benji was inspired by the writing of his aunt's employer. Her knowledge was always all encompassing, which the boy noticed in every conversation. "Oh you know, I think your flowers in front of the house are so beautiful and I'm seriously considering becoming a gardener," he giddy at the two women. Questioningly, they looked into each other's faces. Mary shrugged her shoulders. "The boy wants to be a gardener? I don't believe it," Mary spoke quietly to herself as she put away the dishes in the kitchen. All in all, there was a lot of fun with Ava and Mary in the house again. Ava, meanwhile, still hadn't been able to finish her novel. Even though she had set her mind so firmly on it, she couldn't find a conclusion to her work. The right time to open up and reveal herself was still not there for the already eighty-year-old woman. All of her novels up to that point had always been written in the same way. Same characters, same plot lines, same ending. Her inhibition to write down the reappraisal of her personal history in this novel was simply too great until now. Every day she sat in her office trying to come up with a different ending, but she couldn't. She fell into old writing patterns. If there was one thing she was in her life, it was brave. But apparently not brave enough to show herself to the world. Her personal fate still lay like a secret deep within her and was not yet to be unearthed.

The next day, there was again hustle and bustle at Ava's house. Some women from the town had gathered relief supplies for the needy from the surrounding area. They painstakingly packed everything together in boxes. The volunteers of the aid organization had known each other for a long time, but all too private and intimate things stayed away until now. Ava always made her large house available for this purpose when the aid organization's rooms were occupied. The volunteers gratefully accepted Ava's rooms. The living room, the entire hallway and parts of the kitchen were full of boxes, food and hygiene items for the needy on the street. And because the ladies were so good, Mary baked her world-famous cookies three days earlier. These were to be lovingly packaged in little bags and given to each needy person on the street. For some people out there, being delivered by Ava and Mary was the highlight. They had never experienced such kind gestures from anyone else. There was always something to do with them and that was a good thing. Benjamin, Mary's nephew, also came over to help. His parents were not the wealthiest under the Mississippi sun either, and yet he had learned from Ava and Aunt Mary to always do good, because then good should happen to you as well. His aunt had taught him this wisdom as a child: "If you help others and thus do good, then be praised and go to heaven. Let the best things in life happen to you, too." And after all, who doesn't want the best for their life? Benji always gave full effort in every volunteer activity. He was young, full of vigor and blessed with a lot of power. This carried him through life as far as possible without any major worries. That it would come differently, he did not know until now.

While the women packed the boxes with much love, a touch of soul and gospel surrounded their hearts. Miss Simpson raised her voice and began to belt out a gospel song. One by one, the other women joined in the song. Their powerful voices nearly broke Ava's kitchenware. Benjamin immediately got goosebumps, this was a reason for him why he was completely right in this place; in this sacred place. All the people helped together and had a good time with heavenly singing and delicious cookies. "Hey, the cookies are for the needy. Don't eat them all up!" scolded Mary energetically. Everyone laughed, because after all, if you do something for others, you should be allowed to reward yourself once in a while. Between "Precious Lord" and "Oh happy Day" there was nibbling and laughing. The only one who unfortunately couldn't sing that well was the hostess herself. "Ava, you can do just about anything, but you can't sing like us black folks," grinned her best friend Mary with a conscience that this fact didn't bother Ava. "Ava has a black heart, it's just her voice wouldn't sing along," Miss Simpson joked. Ava gave the ladies a hug. "I apologize Miss Mary. I don't mean to offend you with this question, but why haven't you married and had children before now?" All of a sudden, silence fell and all eyes turned to Mary. But since she had learned to answer difficult questions skillfully, the next sentences were no problem for her. And besides, she was always known for her big mouth. "Well, you know ... Ava is my family. I feel very comfortable here. And of course I have my sister, her husband, and my nephew Benji. They're all my family. That's all I need."

The answer seemed authentic to everyone present, so it didn't require any further questions. Even the most curious among them, Miss Green, had no comment or quip to add. It was all clear; to everyone in the room and Mary had not pretended, but answered honestly and sincerely. "We live in the here and now. I can decide everything for myself and I'm mighty proud of that," the hardworking housekeeper added, shutting everyone's mouths. The freedom to think and act like this is something that some of the women among them would have liked to have for their own lives. But marriage, housekeeping, having children, and work had become the dreary daily routine for many. Mary was neither wealthy nor married, did not have children, nor was she an executive in a company. She had been the black housekeeper of a white, wealthy woman who was a successful writer for quite some time. That's how everyone had seen her: Mary with a big mouth, never letting anyone get her down, and standing up for her opinions. Still, she was the employee of a white woman. And then in the evening, she would drive back to her neighborhood to stop into her little apartment. Yes, that's what they all thought. All the more beautiful and partly unimaginable for the others were those answers that Mary chose glibly but thoughtfully. Because in truth, everyone could see that Mary and Ava had become friends over the years, even best friends. Ava lived a secluded life, was secretive and never let anyone get close to her. But Mary was able to break the ice after all this time. You could see and hear the two of them laughing, this also attracted other people and of course nephew Benji. It was clear Mary didn't want to be married and have children at all. She was happy as she lived and did not want to exchange this. She felt comfortable. There were also times of envy and jealousy among the honorary women, but not in this case. Mary was liked by everyone and currently even highly respected, because she lived true freedom. And this despite the fact that she was cleaning someone else's dirty laundry. All this could never affect her value as a human being. Such attitude she internalized and embodied skillfully. Year after year, day after day. Everything she did, she did with an upright walk and head held high. Her opinion and attitude impressed the other women. A forty-year-old who consciously decided against marriage and children was still something very special, despite all the female emancipation. But she set herself free from what had to be done, in today's world. "I decide for myself and that's fine," was all she added. With that, everything was said. And although she and Ava looked, lived and worked totally differently, they had more in common than anyone suspected. Both women lived independently and self-determined lives, without husbands or children, and both had discovered in their own way the self-confidence to get along for themselves. They were not declared to be the target of the others, but managed it well that their house was visited almost daily by visitors. The two women visibly enjoyed this state of affairs. In the evening, when all the boxes were loaded into a truck and distributed among the people for distribution by the other group of volunteers, Ava's house gradually emptied. Mary put on her jacket, picked up her bag and was about to leave for home when Ava took her in her arms and hugged her tightly. She looked deep into her eyes and whispered softly to hers, "You're my family, too." With tears in her eyes, Mary gratefully left. She had not expected this friendly declaration, despite their good relationship. Happy and full of life, she went out of the house and was never to return ...

The way home turned out to be difficult that evening. It had become dark in the meantime. All too long the women had spent in their charitable work. Miss Simpson offered to take Mary home by car. But proud as she was, she still wanted to take the bus. After all, she could do well out there on the roads. That evening, some cars were driving particularly wildly and aggressively. 'Always these car races. Can't they just let it go?' Mary was getting upset inside. More and more cars were crowding the Mississippi streets in the after-work traffic. One faster than the other. There was speeding and honking. Some drivers wanted to prove their speed and coolness and drove too fast. Everyone knew that such speeding was forbidden, and yet some of the men did not comply.

Gosh, these guys always have to defend their territory, it's annoying, and on their well-deserved day off,' Mary thought to herself. Not looking for a second, a sports racer almost ran off the road while speeding and landed on the sidewalk. "Hey watch it," Mary screamed at the top of her lungs. Totally startled, she jumped to the side and had to stop at the edge of the sidewalk for a few seconds before continuing on to the bus stop. The sports car had long since left and the traffic continued seamlessly, so no one took any notice of this incident. A trifle, people called such a thing among the speeders. Mary, who was usually in such a good mood, suddenly felt uncomfortable. She just wanted to hurry home and enjoy the rest of her evening. Maybe she wanted to soak in a hot bath later and then watch her favorite cooking show on TV? That sounded good, so she decided to do that right at home. Because she had been helping around Ava's house for so long, she was running late. She knew that her bus could come at any moment and leave right under her nose. So she had to hurry, because she didn't want to wait for the next bus. But fate did not mean well for her. The bus pulled up to the bus stop, opened the door, people got off and others got on. Still on the other side of the street, Mary said aloud to herself, "Oh no. Take me with you. I'm coming!" She thought the bus would leave without her, so she ran carelessly into the busy street. It came as it was bound to come. A car, unable to brake as quickly, drove straight at Mary. A split second she noticed that a car was heading towards her. Full of panic, she started screaming. It was too late, the car could not stop and crashed into her with a loud bang.

5.

The world stood still for a moment. The driver got out of his car as fast as he could and walked towards the unknown woman in shock. Mary was lying on the road, covered in blood and motionless. The driver was beside himself and began to cry solidly; he was in a state of emergency. Responsibly, he tried to resuscitate the woman who had been hit. Some passers-by came to the rescue and made an emergency call. The other cars on the road also stopped. Some just stared. Others remained sitting in their cars, waiting for the road to become passable again. Only a fraction of people went to the scene of the accident to administer first aid. The person who caused the accident tried to stop the bleeding, talked to Mary and started to give cardiac pressure massage. He himself was covered with Mary's blood, fear was on his face as well as tears running down his cheeks. He felt incredibly sorry. "Oh my God, oh my God, please stay alive!" he screamed at Mary quite loudly. He became more hasty and moved faster and faster. A woman relieved him and tried her best. The man stood by, paralyzed and apathetic. Every driver's nightmare had turned into reality for him. The police came to the scene and an ambulance was also present a short time later. Needles, syringes, swabs and a defibrillator were used. The emergency physicians worked swiftly and with high concentration. The entire professional staff did their best to keep Mary alive. Were they going to succeed? Everything was still open. The person who caused the accident kept saying, "I'm so sorry. I didn't mean for this to happen. She was suddenly standing in the road." At the same time, he cried bitterly. He could not say more, repeating several times that he was sorry. "She needs to go to the hospital urgently," one paramedic called out to the other. And then everything happened very quickly. Mary, who no longer moved, said nothing and whose eyes were already half closed, did not notice much of all this. She was pushed into the ambulance with the transport stretcher, secured and connected to the life-saving equipment. The ambulance departed with its lights on, and the driver who had hit Mary was still receiving emotional care at the scene.

Once at the hospital, Mary fought for her life. And since she was always a fighter throughout her life, her body tried to fight against the severe injuries and damage caused by the accident. In the operating room, even more doctors and assistants came together to save the injured woman's life. Fortunately, the assistants who had to treat such cases every day were not emotionally attached to the patient. They concentrated on keeping an unknown person alive. For quite a while, no one wanted to give up, and especially not the strong Mary. Only sometimes a higher power played the more significant role in a person's fate. While Mary was lying there, her spirit liked to say goodbye to her and slowly rose invisibly into the sky. Night had fallen in the meantime. It was strangely quiet in the operating room. An hour later, in the middle of the night, Ava's phone rang. Unknowingly, she answered the phone ...

"I understand. Still, I can't believe it. She was here just a few hours ago, wasn't she? We'll be in touch. Thank you for calling," Ava answered a person on the phone. The writer laid the receiver down and silently burst into tears. She grabbed her heart and began to cry from the silence. She screamed as loud as only the deepest pain could make her scream. The other person on the phone was Mary's sister, who told her that Mary had just died in the hospital. And she reported how it happened. That Mary had been hit by a car while crossing the street and that unfortunately it had not been enough for Mary. In her yellow robe, Ava leaned against the wall and slumped down. Sitting on the floor, she asked herself, "Why? Why Mary? Why is someone I love leaving me again?" Until the next morning, she sat on the cold floor in her yellow robe and lit a candle for her best friend. Deep pain and sadness entered the hearts of Mary's family and her best friend, Ava. Mary did not have many close contacts, but this small number of people loved Mary all the more.

The attempt to save Mary's life had failed at the hospital. After a brief rest for all the doctors and assistants, the real work was about to begin. Mary was a good person and wanted to continue doing good for humanity even after her death. Years ago, she decided that if she ever died prematurely, her organs should be available to medical services. She made a cross at organ donation and thus offered her healthy organs to another person. She always carried her organ donor card in her purse, along with her other important documents and some change. Her sister knew that Mary had chosen this path. All that mattered to her was that Mary could expect an honorable burial. The hospital staff and the senior physician entered all the important medical information about Mary together into the database and stored it. The processing time was several hours and required a high level of concentration. The doctors handled the data very sensitively because, after all, this was a recently deceased person. Mary was middle-aged and had always been healthy, so finding a recipient for Mary's organs should not have been difficult. While the lead physician entered the information into the database, the deceased was checked up and down and examined thoroughly. This process took a long time. The accident had damaged some of the internal organs of the woman, who was still so young. But one organ wanted to live on and fought steadfastly to the end. Her heart was stable against all odds and would be ready to be transplanted into another person. Mary was brain dead, yet she had a healthy heart, this was revealed in subsequent tests. Luck of the draw, this seemed to be. The still living heart was like a gift or a kind of loan. Her heart wanted to go on. If only to live on in another person.

Mary's sister, husband and son Benji had arrived at the hospital by now. Completely overtired, in mourning and full of adrenaline, they wanted to see Mary after her serious fatal accident. Benjamin in particular was suffering enormously from the loss of his beloved aunt. What would happen next? The visits to her and Ava gave the young man inner peace and tranquility. He always felt comfortable there and could learn a lot from both women. In addition, the much-visited house was lively and fun. A contrast to some other Mississippi counties. What would Ava's house be like without the best housekeeper in the entire state of Mississippi? What would it be like to never hear Mary's laughter and saucy sayings again? Would he still be welcome at Ava's now that his aunt was no longer alive? Benjamin never felt so bad in his entire life, he would have loved to die along with his aunt. His parents' love and desire to live kept him going. 'I will try for you Aunt Mary here on earth to live on in your spirit,' Benji spoke in his mind to his sorely missed aunt. Then they were finally allowed to see her. The doctor interrupted his examinations and left the room. Slowly, and very hesitantly, they walked toward Mary. Benji's mother grabbed her mouth to prevent an outcry of anger and bewilderment. Her husband, meanwhile, stood at her side. Benjamin had big, thick tears running down his cheeks. At first he didn't dare to look at her and was advised by his father that he didn't have to. But he had to look at her, he wanted to see what she looked like after the accident and would it show? Mary was lying there like an angel. Benji's mind was racing with the idea of how the accident had happened? His aunt was hurt and this thought was unbearable for Benjamin. Condolences were offered to the family from all the hospital staff. After seeing Mary again, they had to go to the police station to get the report of the accident explained. They blamed themselves incredibly after the police report, why none of them drove Mary home by car after the long day of work and volunteering. But it was too late for that now. The accusations should remain accusations and they also knew that Mary did not want help. To be independent and self-determined was her motto in life. She refused any help, even that evening. That evening that was to extinguish her life. The driver who caused the accident was also at the police station. Rarely had they seen a man so desperate for forgiveness. They knew Mary had forgiven him, so they wanted to forgive him, too. Hate would not bring them back either, everyone in the family agreed. Benjamin's parents were very devout. Faith accompanied them throughout their lives. "Thou shalt forgive," a verse in the Bible says. The family wanted to adhere to this and forgave the person who caused the accident, who could hardly believe he was receiving so much understanding. He had expected hatred and violence in his direction, but none of that occurred. He put a letter of apology in

Mary's sister's hand before saying goodbye and leaving the police station through the hallway lit by neon lights. After looking one last time at the accident photo of their sister, sister-in-law and aunt, they also left the police headquarters. The next day, the road led them in the direction of Ava's house. Arriving there, it was still the same building, but nothing was as before, just nothing. The sun was shining from the sky, as if nothing had happened yesterday. The house shone as ever in white splendor and the flowers at the entrance were glowing. For Benjamin, the house of his aunt's best friend was never the same. 'How on earth can the sun be shining today and everything be going its usual way, while I can't understand the world anymore because of pain?' Benjamin didn't even like to enter the house and look into all those faces that seemingly wouldn't understand him. "Now come on in. We're waiting for you," Benjamin's mother was waiting at the entrance. Then he gave himself a jolt and started up the first step. Each step up to the house became more painful for the twenty-five year old young man. Once inside, he didn't dare look Ava in the eye, because he didn't want to admit that that look would mean they had lost a loved one. He wanted to suppress it and not admit it, but Ava beat him to it. She walked straight up to him and hugged him. Without saying anything, she lingered in the position for a few seconds before letting go of Benjamin again. The affection did him good, the silence was like an outspoken sign of compassion. Many neighbors, friends, church members and relief volunteers sat in the living room of Ava's house and shared their sympathy with the family. None of them could believe it. Hadn't they been packing boxes, singing and telling stories with Ava just yesterday? It was a nightmare no one thought possible. Dressed in black, they dedicated a memory session to Mary. Ava placed a large black and white photo of her best friend in a white frame and lit candles around it. That photo had not been taken by her, but by Benji long ago. Mary's beauty was evident in every millimeter of the picture. And if you looked at it closely, the meaning of that black and white photo had a double story to tell. The best friends were different in their skin colors, and yet they were united by a deep bond of eternal friendship. The crowd remained silent until the pastor said a prayer and then they sang gospel together. Many positive things were said about Mary and each person present had an anecdote to add. The only one who didn't want to say anything because he couldn't was Benjamin. His parents didn't leave his side. Ava and Benji kept looking into each other's bleak eyes, as if their souls were connected. At home in the evening, Benjamin didn't sleep a wink. He stayed awake, staring at the ceiling, wondering if his aunt would have it good in heaven now? And he kept asking himself the why question? "Try to sleep, or you'll go crazy. She wouldn't have wanted you to torture yourself like that," his mother tried to soothe him. Eventually, Benji finally fell asleep.

Meanwhile, at the hospital, the decision was made to give Mary's healthy heart to a transplant. The lead physician was adamant about continuing after a long shift to search for a suitable recipient for Mary's heart in the database. The medical information about the woman who died much too soon had to match any genetic medical information, such as the recipient's blood work. With many people across the U.S. in need of donor organs, the attending quickly found what he was looking for. The nurses prepared the OR so the doctors could get started as quickly as possible. Minutes were at stake here; more importantly, life and death. Time could not be wasted. Several doctors stepped up for this important surgery. This was to be the last operation on Mary's lifeless body before she could be buried. Her heart was removed in a long, complicated operation. Clean, neat and highly focused, the organ was successfully removed and would now begin its long journey to the nearest state.

6.

One hour earlier in Louisiana, USA

"Winner of the lottery," one doctor said to the other as he rose from his chair. "I'll contact Mississippi and clarify how soon it can be here." After conferring among colleagues, all the necessary preparations for the organ transplant were made in the operating room. Isabella, who barely had the strength to stand up, felt the ever-approaching movements in the hallway moving toward her room. And she realized that as soon as the door opened, there was a feeling inside her that this time she would not hear that the doctors still had not found a suitable heart for her. It took time for the door to open.

"Please tell me something positive. Please, please, please," Isabella drew on the power of her self-talk. She just stared in the direction of the door. "Go ahead. Door open," she said quietly to herself. She heard the doctor speaking outside the door, it took him a minute to actually open the door all the way and step inside. "A very good day to you Isabella. Your parents are not here yet? We had called them to come. Then I'll be right back," as quickly as he came, the attending physician left. 'What was that supposed to mean? To wish a wonderful good day with a glow on your face and then my parents should come too, although they are here every day', the young patient did not understand, but her intuition had not let her down. She sensed, before the doctor came in, that this time there would be good news for you. Where did this intuition come from? Isabella was starting to get spooked. First the feeling that wouldn't go away, that her heart was missing someone and then her grandmother became an issue again. Then the hospital stay during which she almost died, the endless wait for a donor heart, and now she sensed from the footsteps in the hallway that something good was coming. What did it all mean? As quickly as her parents arrived at the hospital, they had never been there before. 'Can they fly? Isa was stunned and amazed. All the excitement was making itself felt inside her. She felt in her heart that everything was just getting too much. Most of all, she wanted to sleep. But she decided to stay awake. After all, she felt that something had to be said to her and her parents. Did the doctors finally find a suitable heart for her? What she didn't know, her new heart should already be on its way to her. And not just any heart, but a very special one. She was aware of the importance of the donor heart. When she had to wait so long and was told that this was her last hope, she was grateful for every day she was allowed to live, even if only in the hospital. She would rather have been at home in her room, gossiping at length with Katy about his fellow student. It all made her appreciate the moment. Moments come and go, nothing is forever. The most personal moments are the most precious in life.

Then her parents came rushing into the room and looked expectantly into their daughter's eyes. Annabelle and Thomas seemed relaxed, as if no one could touch them today. What would it all mean? "Dad, you must be working or why are you here too?" Isabella looked at her father questioningly. "I don't want to miss this moment," he said clearly. Isa was getting more and more nervous. 'What was different today than yesterday and why this fuss?" she wanted to know. Annabelle didn't say much, Isabella realized that something was up. Everyone around her was acting strange. So was her gut feeling that was about to go on a roller coaster. "Today is the day we've been waiting for for so long. Let's see what exactly the doctors are about to tell us," Thomas added. And then the time finally came. Two of the attending doctors came into Isabella's hospital room in good spirits and cheerful. "For one it is shadow, for the other it is light," the doctor began to philosophize and rambled. Then he continued, "One person has to die so that another can live on." The bitter truth was served to Isabella and her parents on a silver platter. There was no way to sugarcoat such a process, at least not for Isabella. She always hoped, of course, to find a donor organ and thus have a still healthy heart transplanted into her body from a dead person. Neither she knew the person nor his life story or why this person had died? During the long wait, there was a period of guilty conscience. Someone had to die so that she could go on living. Isa was tormented by this thought. 'This is so selfish of me. If there is a donor heart for me, I can't possibly accept it. Someone died and then I'm going to carry on their heart? Somehow I feel complicit and responsible for their death,' the young patient was just thinking way too much in a negative sense. That even her best friend Katy often said lately that Isabella should take distance from these unbearable self-reproaches. Otherwise, her body would reject the newly transplanted heart and her recovery process would be unnecessarily protracted. Isabella continued to daydream.

Meanwhile, the doctor's philosophical speech continued, of which even her parents had to try not to fall asleep. On the one hand, the twenty-year-old, who due to her chronic heart muscle inflammation hardly retained a chance of life without a suitable donor heart, rejoiced. On the other hand, the heart transplant made her feel so bad about herself that she basically didn't want to hear from the attending physician that the vital operation was finally going to take place. She perceived everything as if in slow motion and ignored the doctor's words. Her parents were still sitting there excitedly holding their daughter's hand, this she only caught out of the corner of her eye. She blanked out everything around her and concentrated only on herself. A moment later she felt a jolt, the bed shook. And again she perceived everything in slow motion. Her parents both jumped in the air with joy, stretched their arms upwards and hugged both doctors. Thomas, the father of the terminally ill young woman, had tears standing in his eyes, he was not uncomfortable and he did not wipe them away with a handkerchief. Then her parents embraced her with joy. It was only from this moment that Isabella gradually opened her hearing again. It must have been good news, because everyone present in the room, except herself, rejoiced enormously. "Child, this is wonderful. After waiting for so long, finally ...", her mother seemed to be completely beside herself. There was hasty and jumbled speech and again and again she heard hearty congratulations in her direction. Isa assumed that the philosophizing doctor finished his emotional speech after the other doctor most likely nudged him confusingly to get to the end so he could finally say, "Hooray, a donor has been found and you can have surgery." That could have been had faster, according to Isabella's opinion. The two doctors shook her hand and repeated their congratulations before leaving the hospital room again. "This is great, isn't it? You've been given a second life and I'm so grateful. How are you doing with the news?", Thomas asked his daughter. 'How am I doing? I'm happy, but I'm terrified, so I'd rather not have the surgery, and besides, someone had to give up their life for me just so I could go on living. That's unfair!' Isabella wanted to shout her thoughts out loud so that everyone could hear, but she decided to go for this option: 'Great. I'm excited and can't wait," as she secretly crossed her fingers. "My prayers have been answered. God, thank you," Annabelle looked up and started a conversation with the Lord to say thank you. The whole day, especially the last hour, was most exhausting for the sick woman and she noticed that she was not well despite the joyful news. Her physical condition deteriorated to a low level, which could not be lower while alive. A short time later, unfortunately, Isabella still did not get her well-deserved rest, because now everything had to happen very quickly. She was lying on the hospital bed and could hardly move on her own due to exhaustion. Preparations were made for the difficult and complicated operation. In the process, all the specialists at the hospital noticed that Isabella's condition was getting worse by the hour. "She's going to die on us here alive if we don't start the transplant soon," she heard the doctor, who had just been so motivated, speak from the next room. Isa and her parents still had to sign some important forms. On them was written that she could die during the operation or from the consequences. Or that she would have to be put into a coma. Option three was titled late sequelae, in which case disability could not be ruled out. She realized that she had no choice and that her options were limited. It was difficult for Isabella to sign the forms, because her body soon stopped cooperating, she noticed with every beat of the clock. Her own clock slowly stopped beating and she gradually began to lapse into rigidity. Hoping that when she woke up, it would all be over. The philosophizing doctor told the parents that their daughter was in such a bad condition that there was no guarantee of a good ending. "It all depends on her

74

now. Only on her. She has to want it and her body should accept the foreign organ in the best case. We operate and do our best. But her will must be present for this to succeed," the doctor spoke softly and slowly to the worried parents. The operating room was prepared, also some checks and tests were performed on Isabella before she was then pushed into the operating room. Her last thought before the anesthesia was for her unknown grandmother.

The heart transplant was in full swing. First, doctors removed Isabella's heart from her body. Then, the donor heart was connected to the vena cavae of the pulmonary artery and the aorta of Isabella as the recipient. The heart, which was still biologically active, was to continue to live, work and throb in Isabella's body. However, heart transplantation was a profound procedure fraught with significant risks, and if Isabella had not been exposed to such high risk, doctors would have weighed their decision differently. The immunosuppressive therapy required brought with it the risk of inflammation because the immune system is severely compromised in the process. Meanwhile, the heart-lung machine was working at full speed. After several hours, it was finally done. The heart transplantation was successfully completed and Isabella continued to receive intensive care. The parents of the newly operated patient were relieved when they were informed that the operation had gone well.

7.

Mississippi, USA

Where there was joy in Louisiana over the successful heart transplant, the world seemed to stand still in Mississippi. "I think the pain from all over the United States of America is in this house today," Mary's sister spoke to Ava. The latter nodded and remained introverted. At 80 years old, the deceased's best friend kept her feet bravely and valiantly. She had still worked hard in the past, lovingly and caringly tending to her lush front yard and co-leading the volunteer relief effort for those in need in the area. At her age, she should have been taken care of, but Ava was a secretive personality who only opened up to Mary about private matters. But she had unfortunately left before her. Who could have guessed that? It was noticeable that the funeral visits did not take place in Mary's small apartment or in her sister's living quarters. The mourners' meetings took place at the home of the fair-skinned Ava, who, more accurately, was Mary's employer. Mary did not live with Ava, nor did Benjamin, although he visited often. These facts were not to matter; for the white house, surrounded by colorful flowers, was the place where Mary, during her lifetime, spent most of her time and was exceedingly comfortable there. Although the house was filled with life and visitors almost every day, the deceased had only a few people whom she really trusted. So it surprised no one that her sister, his husband and Ava decided to hold a small funeral service soon in Mary's spirit. "She probably wouldn't have agreed to a grand exit," was one of the few phrases Ava uttered. She didn't want to intrude on other family matters; so far, she found most of the words to clarify in her novels. She was intelligent and intellectual; accordingly, she would have had a lot to say. But just like Mary, Ava never wanted to stand out in the crowd. She knew that now that she had a very good friend and confidante by her side for so long, such a friendly relationship would most likely not happen again in her life. And that was perfectly okay with her. At 80 years old, to completely open up to a stranger again, she could not imagine right now and to be honest, she had no need for it. Even before her employee was buried, she decided to spend the last stage of her life on her own, preferably without depending on anyone. Benji, of course, was still welcome at her place, if he wanted to come. She was sad, but also very grateful for the time with Mary and the memories they shared. Would she be able to finish her novel this way?

In the afternoon, when the sun glowed orange-yellow and the rays represented a connection between heaven and earth for Ava, she sat in her front yard and created a large, colorful flower wreath. This was so aesthetically and delicately put together that a florist could not have done it better. So obsessed with giving her friend a final greeting, she didn't go to bed that night, but continued creating the large wreath until the next morning. The night was hot and the lights at Ava's house, which she needed to work, shone so brightly that a swarm of mosquitoes gathered around the old lady and she carried away a souvenir the next morning. Tired and full of mosquito bites, she put the wreath of flowers in the cool basement and disappeared into her bedroom. A few hours of sleep did her good. 'The last time I pulled an all-nighter, gosh it's been a long time.' Memories of days gone by returned to her. She skillfully ignored the neighbors' ringing. She didn't want a visitor right now. Not to communicate, just to sleep. Even if the freshly brewed and brought coffee of the neighbors penetrated upstairs through the open bedroom window, she remained persistent and fell asleep ...

Some time later, Mary's family came by Ava's house again. They held a meeting earlier with the pastor about the funeral ceremony. "Ava?" they repeated. The family called loudly through the large house, but no one responded. "Honey, you check the basement. Benji, you go upstairs and I'll check the back of the house to see if she's there?", Mary's sister distributed the tasks. Benjamin climbed the stairs with restraint. Ava was a fine, fancy lady to him, and he didn't want to disturb her in a private situation. 'Maybe she's just taking a shower, or changing her clothes?' Possibly she's finishing her novel, or worst of all, she's mourning the loss of my aunt?' Benjamin suspected the latter, and therefore reacted inhibitedly to opening the doors on the second floor without Ava asking him to do so. In any case, she was not in her writing room. Then Benji stood in front of the bedroom door, not daring to open it a crack. But not hearing his parents call out that Ava had been found, he tentatively pushed the door away from him and there she lay. Ava was fast asleep. At first Benjamin was startled, because he had never seen her sleeping at noon before. Therefore, his assumption was that she had now passed away as well. But how could he find out? He slowly crept up to the elderly lady and fortunately saw that her chest was slightly heaving as she breathed. Actually, he wanted to disappear back downstairs to let his parents know that she was in the bedroom. But somehow he felt the need to ask Ava if everything was all right with her? "Aunt A ...", Benjamin immediately interrupted his words. He had actually meant to say "Aunt Ava." How could this have happened? Was he so confused and in mourning? Mary was, after all, his only aunt. Ava was the longest and best friend of his aunt Mary, who had died much too soon. He was the nephew of the coolest housekeeper from all of Mississippi and he was proud of that. But why would the word "aunt" slip out of his mouth in reference to Ava? Embarrassing, Benji thought to himself. 'I hope she didn't hear that?", Benjamin's shame rose to the top of his head, his cheeks flushed slightly. He noticed that she was moving and about to wake up. He slowly but quickly slipped out the door and hurried downstairs to his parents. Totally stressed, he sat down on the couch and said totally nonchalantly,

"She's upstairs in her bedroom. Must have been sleeping and just woke up." His parents breathed a sigh of relief. The three of them waited together with a cup of freshly brewed tea for the sleepy one. The next day was to be the funeral of their sorely missed Mary ...

The cloud cover was closing in over Mississippi. It began to rain. The sky wept, now an angel had ascended to them far too soon. Was this to be, they wondered? As Mary would have wanted, there were few guests at her funeral. Her only sister and brother-in-law, her beloved nephew Benjamin, Doctor Houston Jr, a few neighbors, and of course her best friend Ava. Everyone was dressed in black, although Mary never thought much of dress codes. Ava kept an upright gait for her 80 years, but her heart was broken. She had already been through a lot in her life that no one knew about. Much of it she dealt with herself. Benji was supported left and right by his parents. He too was in mourning throughout for what he considered the best aunt he could have ever asked for. The atmosphere remained silent, no one said anything except for the pastor.

"Dear mourners, dear relatives, dear neighbors, dear friends!

We are gathered here today on this rainy day to say goodbye. Farewell to a kind-hearted person. Lord God, you took her to yourself far too soon for those who love her. Only you can know why? Mary, you were a strong personality and had many talents. You never kept your opinions to yourself, but you never imposed yourself with your words. You are still a child of God who is now embarking on what will probably be your last journey. You always worked hard and yet nothing was too much for you. You listened to the problems of others and often gave wise advice. You shall shine. Your light shall shine like the light of God on earth and give strength to those who mourn you. For your volunteer work you are praised and glorified in singing Hallelujah. You came to church, you were part of the congregation. God spoke in your voice in gospel singing. To many out there, you were a role model because you were different. You never chose to tie the knot or bring children into the world. But you lived every day of your life in love. Strong as a lioness and free as a bird you were. Your short life had a meaning. You were an asset and a help to many people who now sorely miss you. As Mary's sister told me, the deceased was a fan of the song "I love Rock and Roll." And I hope for your understanding that we cannot have the song played for her here at the cemetery. Perhaps later, in private and at a later hour, you can do her that favor? [The mourners begin to laugh, although they have tears in their eyes.] We now want to say goodbye to the wonderful Mary and pray for her together ...May the Lord grant her eternal peace. Amen."

After the cemetery visitation and official burial, the mourners in attendance returned to Ava's home. Mary's sister told stories of her from the 40 years she had lived. She shared many funny anecdotes about the housekeeper, which lightened the mood among the other guests. Then she wanted her son to come forward to say something about his aunt as well. With a wave of her hand, she invited him to stand up here in front. Embarrassed, Benji remained sitting on the couch until his father pushed him up with his hands behind his back. Slowly, he walked toward his mother and had to take a deep breath. The others clapped their hands. Except Ava didn't. She sensed that the boy didn't want to. But then he opened his mouth, everyone looked at him expectantly. He already didn't like big speeches at school. That's why he kept it short and sweet, saying only, "I miss you!" These three words not yet completely pronounced, he sat down already again on the couch. The others looked irritated because of the brevity of his speech, but they clapped anyway. After all, what could be better than just saying straight out that you missed someone? Ava also applauded him for that. Then it was her turn. As a best friend, she would certainly have had a lot to say. But it was not her style to talk out of the closet. She wanted to keep the respect for Mary and gave a speech about Mary in the best sense of the word: "When she started working for me as a housekeeper many years ago, there was not exactly approval in the neighborhood. Silly sayings and nasty looks were on the increase. When people noticed that the two of us also got along well, we were often told through the grapevine that friendships between black and white don't work. They were trying to tell us that it must not work! We had both been different, but with the same view. Friendship was allowed to exist everywhere and no one had the right, really no one, to break us apart. First they said that the black woman could work for me, but that no friendship should result from it. Respect was okay, but we both had respect for each other, that bonded us. At some point I realized that she was such a good person that even if I had told her a secret, she would never have told anyone. Such certainty did me good; did me good. She would take the secret with her to the grave and that is why she will remain my best friend for all eternity. This was finally noticed by the last people in our environment and the slandering stopped as quickly as it had come. On the contrary, we two were recognized and appreciated by the people. From that day on, my house was full of guests and I had little privacy." Ava smirked at her own words, producing a laugh. Everyone knew that as a writer, she needed quiet. For work, she usually retreated to her writing room. And yet she and Mary were so popular that they actually had little privacy left because their house was full of visitors almost every day. This state of affairs remained so until Mary's death. After Ava's speech, there was a brief silence, her words stimulating everyone present to think. Racism was still an issue in the U.S., then and now. None of the mourners knew about the fact that the beginnings of this special friendship were difficult. Everyone always thought there had never been any problems. People can be wrong sometimes, as this example showed. "All that glitters is not gold," Mary's brother-in-law interjected. "If we had let each other make us insecure as a duo, we never would have had this friendship. And we would have missed the best time of our lives just because others wanted us to. Society often demands living a life that conforms to values Mary and I didn't share. Against all odds, we continued to talk privately and never let ourselves be oppressed. She was very special, even her taste in music was slightly special," Ava spoke as she went to the CD player and put in "I love Rock and Roll." Probably the only song that had ever been played at a funeral service to date. Everyone in attendance sang and danced for Mary. Her life and memory were honored. No one was to forget her and the life she lived. And certainly not her funeral service. This is what the deceased would have wished for.

8.

Louisiana, USA

Isabella gently woke up from anesthesia. Opening her eyes, she looked into the faces of her parents. What a loving sight and happiness to have woken up again, Isabella felt. The heart transplant took hours, so the day was almost over. Her parents wore blue gowns and mouth guards, because Isa was to be accompanied and cared for in the intensive care unit for a long time. The operation was complicated and risky. Isabella was still tired from the anesthesia, the long surgery and the surgery itself. She felt pain and was totally weakened. She also noticed that her entire chest didn't feel the same as before. She had been very unwell in the past, but the pain she was in from the surgery was extreme. Her body was not the same as before, her sick heart was replaced with a healthy one. So now she was carrying the heart of a deceased person. It felt different, weird and strange; so strange. The pain and effort should be enough for today. At some point she fell asleep and didn't wake up until early the next morning.

The doctors and nurses present were taking care of the young patient in a professional manner. She was still hooked up to the machines and was constantly observed and monitored. Isabella had the pleasure, which was not at all to her liking, of being constantly checked over. Even the smallest negative change, be it fever, abnormal blood values or high blood pressure, could cost her life. She got an all-around; all-inclusive treatment, as one nurse joked with her. Laughter was good, but Isabella needed to move to more of a neutral physical state because laughter took too much out of the body. The nurse was taken aside by a colleague and told about the risks of such jokes in the intensive care unit. 'They shouldn't make such a fuss.' After all, laughter is the best medicine.' Isa had sympathy and understanding for the funny nurse. She was bored. That's why she was happy to receive any kind of encouragement. Still, she noticed that she was physically unable to be funny at the moment. Her heart and the whole area were just still hurting too much. Her parents, of course, came to see her earlier that morning. They were very worried. After all, not every patient had survived the first night after such a serious operation. Overjoyed and joyful, they looked into the eyes of their living and only daughter. The doctor who operated on her was also there to tell Isabella and her parents once again about the successful operation and about her current condition: "The phase immediately after transplantation is critical and must not be underestimated, nevertheless the patient makes a solid impression as long as one can say that now. Keep it up." The doctor left the room. Was the doctor talking about her just now? A solid impression she made? Isabella didn't quite understand. She felt as if she had been run over by a train. There was no question of "solid" in her case. "When do I get to see

Katy and Jack? And when will I find out who this heart once belonged to? I'm dying to know. No, I must know!" The sick woman asked many questions and made many demands. Her parents didn't even know how to answer all the questions? Annabelle and Thomas looked at each other regretfully. "Honey, you are not related to Katy and Jack. They can't visit you in the ICU. I'm afraid you'll have to wait until you're transferred to the regular ward. That depends solely on your condition and how you accept the foreign heart. And who the donor is, we have to ask the senior attending," her mother replied. "Yes mom. Then please ask. I can't wait that much longer. I really need to know now." Isabella cared deeply about the subject. Her father Thomas joked, "Why can't you wait that long anymore? Where are you going and what are you planning to do? Have you been invited to a party?" He grinned like a honey-cake horse and promptly received light blows from his wife on his back. "You're not supposed to make her laugh. It's dangerous for her!" Annabelle responded angrily. Her mother was right, after all, but for the second time today she figured a little fun couldn't hurt. And yet, every time she laughed, her entire upper body ached painfully. Her parents got up and wanted to talk to the senior physician again, because of Isabella's demand. It took quite a while until they came back. With wide, expectant eyes, Isa looked at her father and mother. "So ... the attending said that this topic was way too early for you. The hospital staff knows who your donor is. But you can't deal with that right now. As I said, it's way too early. You are in the ICU and recovery will take a very, very long time. And the doctor said the first priority right now is for your body to accept the transplanted heart and not reject it. You need to recover and become one with your donor organ," the mother relayed what she could gather from the doctor. Her father agreed and nodded in the affirmative. Isabella was raging, she was boiling with anger inside and again she realized that this feeling was not good for her body, but she just couldn't help it. She didn't want to lie there clueless, staring at the ceiling and counting the tiles on the wall. She defended herself and would not let this answer stand: "But my recovery can take years and I have to take medication for life. Should I now wait eternal years until I am allowed to know which heart is beating in my body? I can't let that happen, I want to know soon!" The parents looked at each other powerlessly. They knew they had a fighter for a daughter and she would never put up with years of waiting, so they tried to reassure Isabella, "No one says you have to wait for years, but now and for the next few weeks you won't find out from anyone. You have to accept that for the sake of your health. You have been terminally ill, just recently operated on. Now, surely, something else must be more important to you than knowing very quickly who your donor is? I can't understand that." Thomas didn't say anything at all this time, and Isabella was getting angrier by the second. "Or do you want to break into the office at night and secretly look into the database to see which person this heart belonged to?" he hadn't been able to stifle this remark. He himself had to laugh out loud at that, and then Isabella did too. Promptly he received another blow from his wife, this time on the shoulder. An assertive voice replied to the family, "The patient must rest and under no circumstances be disturbed in her recovery by external stimuli!" Thomas bowed his head down, feeling a little ashamed that he had gotten his daughter into such trouble the day after her surgery. As a policeman, he was fair, but also very strict. As a father, on the other hand, he was more in the mood for jokes. Isabella had no choice but to accept that she would not know for a long time to come to whom she owed this heart. For the reason that she almost died shortly before the operation, she stayed in the intensive care unit for two weeks. And again she tried again. Whenever a doctor attended to her alone, she asked about the person who had lent her the heart. In doing so, she acted mischievously, tried to engage people in conversation and was not stingy with compliments. And all this just to get information about her donor. But none of the doctors got involved; they all remained highly professional. Only once, she had been able to almost wrap the shy and kind-hearted nurse Miss White around her finger, if the head physician hadn't come for rounds at the same moment. After that, the opportunity was over, because Miss White had smelled a rat and wouldn't say a word. Her parents provided her with literature every day, which pleased Isabella, who would have preferred to study. After she came down from the ICU, she was allowed to draw in her room. Her parents brought drawing pad and pencils. No one but family was allowed to visit her in her room yet. But every day her parents brought letters and cards from friends for their daughter to cheer her up a little. Attentively she read through each greeting and was delighted that so many dear people kept thinking of her. She was not forgotten, as unfortunately were some others in her ward. She appreciated all of this, including the conversations between her and her friendly bedmate. And because she was young and alive, she had dreams. She wanted to get healthy, if healthy was defined differently from people who didn't have a serious illness. She also wanted to go back home, move around and laugh out loud. To find out who her donor was and, last but not least, to know who her old heart had missed? Would this have been too much to ask? Were the wishes too lofty, too utopian? Would her life have been all about taking medication and somehow getting along with the donor heart? The twenty-year-old dealt with all these questions every day. The daily meals at the hospital were so-so, at least that's how Isabella felt. The senior physician was really nice. He explained to the recently operated patient what would happen in the first months after the operation: "Isabella, this is how it is: After the transplant, the new organ has to start working. Normally, your new heart would be recognized by the body's defense system as foreign tissue and attacked. In principle, you can imagine this as being similar to the incompatibility between different blood groups. Therefore, from the transplantation on, you will have to take medication for the rest of your life to regulate your immune system. This has been explained to you many times. Immunosuppressants are indispensable. Only in this way can the organ be accepted by the body and function ..." And he talked and talked and talked, making Isabella almost dizzy. Even before she was operated on, she knew everything about the surgery, the transplant and what would happen afterwards. She had heard it all explained a thousand times before. Because the doctor was quite nice, she thought it would be rude to interrupt him or even lecture him that she already knew all about it. But because she was Isabella after all and she just felt a little annoyed by the information she had known for a long time, she decided to be annoying now and ask the doctor about the unknown donor again. "Be patient a little longer. It will all work out," having just uttered half a novel, Herr Oberdoktor answered the all-important question only briefly and succinctly. 'Typical man. He bores me beforehand, but then he balks at answering important questions', Isabella thought to herself a little cynically. Another week passed in the normal treatment ward. Her roommate was also still there and they had become friends in the meantime, which contributed greatly to the recovery of both women. Isabella's hope of finally receiving information was gradually fulfilled.

The doctor who had operated on her and who had recently lectured her with a novel about what was happening to her, finally got to the point. Her parents were sitting next to her and neither knew who Isabella's donor was nor that they were now informed about it. The excitement was enormous and visible in Isabella's face. She had last been this active and agile in her features before coming to the hospital.

"Dear Isabella, dear parents of the patient ...", it became even formal. The doctor continued, "Today is the day I tell you who your donor was. Her name was Mary and she was 40 years old before she died. She was in perfect health and from what I was told, a woman full of life. Her skin color is like yours, dark. Unfortunately, she was hit by a car while crossing the street and did not survive this accident. She lived in the neighboring state of Mississippi and had no children or husband, but was still happy all around. She worked as a housekeeper for a white elderly lady and must have been the best cook out of all of Mississippi. She left behind a sister, brother-in-law and also a nephew. On top of that, she volunteered to help the needy in her town. What more can I say? She must have been a good person. This is all the information I have about her. I hope I could fulfill your most ardent wish Isabella with it? And that you can process all the information well for you? If you have any further questions, I am at your disposal. But now I have to go back to the operating room. See you later." The family thanked him sincerely and after the doctor left Isabella's hospital room, they had to cheer briefly but loudly with joy.

"Finally. Now we know who she is. It all sounds good, except for the fact that she passed away," the mother held. The three talked for a while about the now no longer unknown Mary before the parents headed home for the evening. The roommate congratulated Isabella on finally having clarity. 'When I tell Katy and Jack. They'll be curious about the identity of my donor to whom I owe my life,' a greeting and a thank you for her life Isabella sent to Mary up in the sky.

9.

Isabella was continuously in the hospital. Her condition was good according to the circumstances. Now she was finally allowed to receive visitors again, outside of her parents. Good former school friends came to visit her, as did the leader of a sports group to which she had once belonged. Other relatives rejoiced with her immensely that she had survived the operation well. A good friend from the neighborhood also came to visit. All this contributed to the recovery of her immune system. Besides her parents, she was most looking forward to the visit of her best friend Katy and her boyfriend Jack. They hadn't seen each other for a long time; Isa often had the experience that friends change when you don't see them for a while. But this assumption was unfounded, Katy behaved as she always did. She almost freaked out when she saw Isabella again for the first time. Both girls even shrieked with joy, like they were at a concert. "Ladies. Not so loud!" a nurse had to stop the two friends. "I missed you so much, it's good to see you," Katy had tears in her eyes. And then Isabella was busy the rest of the day listening to her friend talk. The hours flew by and it felt like they were sitting in their room at home and not in the hospital. The twenty-year-old listened to everything. From campus to men or slurring about fellow female students. Katy was back in her element. And it did Isabella so much good to listen to her; it made her feel like a normal young woman living a real life. But the truth was different. She had faced death and refused to follow it. After the heart transplant and stay in the ICU, she was now in the regular ward and at the point where she was allowed to have visitors. The next step would be to come home. Even that did not mean freedom for her. If she was home, then she would have to take it easy. She realized that she wouldn't be able to go to the movies or to the gym or spend the night at Jack's right away, as well as two young people in love. It would take a long time for her to come to terms with the medication, and with the foreign organ. So her life path was going to be completely different from that of her best friend Katy. And yet she drew strength from her friend's stories, also to feel that she was still alive. The idea of being able to do all these things again herself one day would be great. After what felt like hours, Isabella finally got around to saying, "I know who she is!" Katy looked cluelessly at Isabella's face and asked who she meant? At first she had in her mind that her heart was missing someone before the hospitalization and now Katy thought that was what it was all about. "No. I know who my donor is. So who I have to thank for the heart," Isabella spoke enthusiastically. Completely surprised, Katy replied, "No Isa. You really know who she is?" Then Isabella pulled out with a bang all the information she herself received from the doctor. She told all about Mary and about the life she had lived on the streets until before the tragic accident. "She must have been a pretty great person and I'm so grateful to her for that heart. For that crazy heart. If that Mary had known what crazy noodle would later carry her organ ...," Isabella added. Both young women then had to laugh out loud. Then Katy got serious, her voice changing from loud to quiet to wary: "How can you think that about yourself? You're not crazy. You're my best friend and I don't think Mary could have imagined anyone else as a recipient better than you." She gave her best friend a big hug.

There wasn't much more to add to that, it had gone quiet around the two of them for a moment that even the nurse had to look to see if they hadn't taken flight? Afterwards, Katy asked, "So, what are you going to do next?" Isabella thought. There was only one thing she was determined to accomplish at the moment. And that had nothing to do with wanting to find out who her old heart was missing? Since she had received a new heart from Mary and had just had surgery, that old feeling was not there at the moment. That's why she answered, "I want to contact Mary's family. Write a letter, contact her sister. And I hope she will answer me and I can meet her one day?" It was spoken. The plan for the near future should surely stand. Making contact with Mary's sister was inevitable for the heart recipient. Katy confirmed her intention and could well relate, "And you know what the good thing is? By connecting with the family of your donor heart, you get to add a new family." Isabella had never thought of it that way before. A new family? She had never thought about that before, but she found the thought pleasant. Her family would expand, with excitement Isabella looked forward to the future. Completely determined and soon into action, she rang her mother on her cell phone in the presence of Katy and asked her to bring stationery, envelope, pen and of course a stamp. Annabelle wasn't sure if this was a good thing to do, but couldn't deny her daughter her wish. Isabella's goal, after all, was to get well. "And now there's just one thing missing," Katy said, "Yeah, what's that?" Isabella was on the edge of her seat, forgetting the most important thing about the letter. "The address. Jeez Isabella. Mary's sister's address in Mississippi. You don't have that yet, do you?" countered her longtime best friend, who thankfully was thinking along. "It's a good thing I have you. I'll take care of the address later," Isabella got serious. But the rest of the time the friends spent talking around Isabella's surgery and Katy's life. There was much laughter and giggling until visiting hours were over and the two said goodbye to each other. The next day during rounds, Isabella asked the doctors for Mary's sister's address. The deceased gave her sister's contact information in Mississippi with her documents around organ donation. Immediately, Isa got the green light and the address would soon follow. Likewise, Annabelle brought everything necessary for her daughter to draft the letter. Lost in thought, Isabella's mind was busy formulating the letter. By mistake, she overlooked the door and almost bumped her head against it, if her roommate had not warned her at the last second. "You think too much and dream too much," was the correct guess of the bright neighbor. She was right, after all, but thoughts were the only place from which she could not be driven. Loosely following this motto, Isabella formulated back and forth in her head, seeing herself at the very first meeting with Mary's sister. 'Would they come visit me in Louisiana? Or am I going to Mississippi? I wonder what it's like there. I've never been there,' the young patient was already skipping the next step. Then all of a sudden the door actually opened, her boyfriend Jack was standing in the doorway. The happiness could not have been greater. After such a long time, the two of them were immensely happy to be able to embrace each other again. The thoughts about the possible end of the relationship were forgotten for Isabella. Everything was good again and that should last for now. "I am so happy to see you. How are you and how are you taking the new organ?" he asked as Isabella made her way to her hospital bed. His girlfriend told him everything except the last and most recent point. She told him about Mary but not that she was about to write to the latter's sister in Mississippi. Interested, Jack listened to everything and told about his life. It came as it had to come. Just in time for tea, the address of Mary's sister was delivered to Isabella. It was placed in a blue envelope. Isabella already suspected that the contact information had been placed in this envelope. "What's that?", Jack wanted to know. Isa pretended it was something unimportant and hid the blue envelope under her pillow. Jack looked funny, because he didn't like Isabella keeping secrets from him. Knowing him as someone who didn't keep so much understanding in the past, she decided not to tell him about it at all. She changed the subject faster than lightning. Meanwhile, her roommate went for a walk in the hallway outside so Jack and Isabella could have some time to themselves. After an hour, as she lay back in her bed, she asked Isabella if she had gotten the address from the doctors yet? Jack was immediately bright eyed and of course wanted to know what the address was? 'Crap. Now Jack won't rest until he knows what's going on. If only the neighbor had kept her mouth shut.' Isabella was annoyed. She didn't want to answer, but like a private detective, he kept managing to follow up until Isabella did tell. She didn't like that about him. He couldn't let anything go and always wanted to get his way. He also did not respect her privacy. She liked him and was grateful for his support, but something inside her said they weren't that good together. "So this is so ...," Isa started to stutter. Her roommate noticed this immediately and wondered, because in all the weeks before she had never noticed Isabella nervous and with speech problems. She suspected that Jack might be responsible. Isabella must have had a valid reason for not wanting to tell Jack about writing to her donor's sister. The neighbor verbally kept her mouth shut. But Jack still wouldn't let up until Isa then told him about the plan to write to Mary's sister in

Mississippi. To say thank you for her new life and, in the best case scenario, to meet Mary's family. 'Don't keep talking. He doesn't deserve it, he's too curious. 'Isa, don't tell him anything more,' the roommate thought intuitively. But Isabella told it like it was her beak. Instead of being happy for his friend, he blamed Isabella for not telling him directly what was in the blue envelope. Isabella almost had to cry, because the accusations against her did not stop. 'If this goes on, I'm about to press the emergency bell so that a nurse or the security guards will put an end to this disaster' her neighbor was very worried about Isabella. She grabbed her heart and decided to put an end to the goings-on herself. She kindly asked Jack to leave the hospital and leave her alone for the time being. Still totally annoyed, he rose, indicated a kiss on Isabella's cheek and immediately withdrew it. Isabella's new friend couldn't stifle a loud: "That's enough insolence now". "You'd better go now," Isabella added confidently. Jack lifted his head up and strutted out the door. "Can't understand why you're with him?" wondered the roommate and new friend. The young, heartbroken woman began to cry bitterly. Jack had never offended her like this before. "It's over. He's gone," her friend took her in her arms. Isabella went to sleep later without having looked into the blue envelope. Isabella was still not to do anything in that direction for the next three days. She realized that she needed to calm down and digest Jack's brief but unpleasant visit for herself. Isa wanted to regain her old strength and vigor. Katy and her parents gave her every opportunity to do so. On the fourth day after Jack's visit, when she found new courage and the visit had just left, she took out the blue envelope. She had hidden it in her room safe by now. Mary's sister's address was sacred to Isabella. The attentive room neighbor delicately noticed that it was time to leave her alone with the letter. That's why she went with her visitor to the hospital cafeteria. Rarely had Isa been so nervous. She sat there for minutes without opening the envelope. What lay inside could change her life. Filled with awe and excitement, she finally opened the blue envelope. Inside was the address of Mary's sister in Mississippi. For another few minutes, she just stared at the address and held the happiness in her hands. She was finally going to use the writing utensils Annabelle had brought her. Toward evening, as it grew slightly dark, she put pen to paper and began to write:

Dear sister of my heart donor. My name is Isabella, I am 20 years old and from Louisiana. A few weeks ago I almost died from my chronic heart muscle inflammation. Thanks to her sister Mary, I am now living on. Without her heart, I would not be on this earth today. I learned what a good person her sister had been, and I can imagine how hard it is to live without her. I'm sure you miss her immensely. I will carry her heart with the greatest respect and try to continue to go through the world with the greatest love in Mary's spirit as well. I would like to get to know you, your husband and your son, to be even closer to Mary. And to learn more about her. I would be happy if this would be possible soon or someday for you and me. I look forward to hearing from you.

With love

Isabella

Before she hopefully sent the letter, she read through the lines several times. And all the time she thought to herself that her words were not good enough for Mary's family. But then she put the letter in the mail after all. From that moment on, she was in constant anticipation of a reply from the deceased's sister. Everyone around her could tell that Isabella was hoping and dreading to receive mail every day. Several weeks passed, and again and again she would ask, "Is there anything for me?" Unfortunately, the letter carrier had to answer in the negative, and Isabella's smile disappeared. "She'll get back to you. I'm sure she just needs some time to do it. Look, she lost her sister and probably can't deal with the recipient of her sister's heart just yet. Be patient, everything will be fine," her father comforted her. A caregiver added that some family members never get in touch; they just don't respond to the people who received an organ from the deceased. "Bitter, but now reality," the young colleague summed it up. Isabella sadly withdrew, but she never gave up hope. Annabelle and Thomas, as well as her best friend Katy, spent their time continuing to support Isabella in her recovery process. In the meantime, she felt very comfortable on the ward, everyone was nice to her and took good care of her. It was often fun, and her roommate had long since become a close friend. She no longer contacted Jack of her own accord; he had made her feel too insecure and bullied her. It did her good not to see him. He, on the other hand, didn't get in touch either. His ego had grown at the same time that he began his studies, which displeased Isabella. "Do you want me to write her another letter? Maybe the first one got lost in the mail and she never received it? Anything is possible," the young patient told herself. Her parents looked at her depressingly and told her to let it go. She was doing well with her heart, and no further complications arose. The medication was a horror for Isabella; she would eventually have to take it for the rest of her life. 'That's a great outlook,' she thought to herself, and would have liked to throw the pills in the garbage can if they weren't vital for her. The next day was finally the day. The long-awaited letter was ceremoniously handed to her by the letter carrier. "I hope this is the letter you've been waiting for so long!" Completely excited, Isabella tore the mail out of the messenger's hand. Since she did not want to be so rude and did not accept this behavior from others, she immediately apologized to the nice gentleman. However, everything was fine. He could understand how important outside contacts were in the hospital. Even her roommate went completely berserk, could hardly wait for the letter, she was so excited. What would the letter say? Was there perhaps already an invitation to Mississippi? And was Mary's sister as kind-hearted as her sister once was? Questions upon questions. Isabella sat comfortably on her bed and was about to open the letter when her neighbor said, "And don't be too disappointed if there's no invitation to Mississippi in the letter." Isabella didn't understand why people were all reacting so negatively to the letter? Because she herself had been looking forward to it for weeks and it meant everything to her. Just as she was about to open the letter, something intervened again. A cheerful and joyful voice in the shape of a nurse announced the next examination for Isabella as if she were selling flowers at the market. Totally annoyed, Isabella put the letter aside, stood up and followed the good-humored woman to the examination. 'Not again. Why does something keep coming up? I want to read the letter' any thoughts turned exclusively to the answer from Mississippi. The young woman was almost obsessed with reading the reply. The examination went well and she was allowed back to her room. Without greeting her neighbor, she rushed to the letter and opened it hastily. She had never opened a letter so quickly. Because the neighbor didn't want to look at Isabella so curiously and conspicuously, she began to read a romance novel in the meantime. Blanking out her surroundings, Isa focused her attention solely on the letter intended for her. She read the first lines and everything was still good. The further down she got in reading the lines, the more her mood dimmed. 'This can't be true. Please don't,' she thought to herself as she continued to read intently. Her state of mind could change so quickly. One minute she was full of anticipation and anticipation, the next she was sad and saddened. Her roommate noticed that the contents of the letter did not meet Isabella's expectations. But she didn't know what to say? She put the romance novel on the bedspread and looked at her newfound friend. She would have been right there to comfort Isabella if she liked it. Isa, meanwhile, continued reading and it was evident on her face that there was nothing positive in the lines. She suppressed her tears and tried to remain steadfast. Then she didn't make a face and patiently read on to the end. Isabella tried to accept what she did not like. That was adult life, apparently. Not always getting what you hoped for. She tried to tell herself this attitude, but it didn't help. Finished reading, she laid the letter aside and said nothing. The tears rolling down her cheeks spoke for her instead. Without a word, her roommate stood up and took Isabella in her arms. She thought it wise not to inquire further either. Her friend should tell her herself, if she felt able to do so. Huddled alone in the bathroom, the tears just poured out of her. And she asked herself the question, why? She grabbed her heart and mentally began to talk to Mary. Half an hour later she left the bathroom and sat down on her bed again. Her parents came to visit and, of course, immediately asked. The feelings were to come out and Isa fell crying into her parents' arms. Although her mother was so eloquent, she said nothing this time and waited until Isabella was ready. "She doesn't want any contact with me. She just doesn't want it. I never come to Mississippi," she said, briefly explaining the contents of the letter. Everyone in the room was dismayed. Then she continued to add, "She's glad I'm doing well. The family accepts my thanks, but that's as far as Mary's sister wants any contact with me." Thomas, Isabella's father, tried to find encouraging words for his daughter, "You have to accept it, put yourself in her shoes. Not everyone can do this. You wrote to her because it was important to you to say thank you. And with that you did everything in your power. You can't influence the rest. She doesn't want to. The best thing you can do now is concentrate on getting along well with Mary's heart." Annabelle gave her husband approval. The words in her father's mouth sounded so simple, but in truth they were not for Isabella. Everyone was taking care of her, which she didn't like. She didn't want the attention and that everything was always about her. Her wish was to be left alone and do her own thing. She had received enough unwanted attention from everyone because of her heart disease. And that's why she often felt guilty. She wished her loved ones would go on with their own lives and not focus so much on Isabella. She just didn't like to carry on like this anymore. Her family and friends had lives of their own. Isabella didn't want to ruin it for them. She was okay, but unfortunately not right now. In order not to burden the others, she decided not to make a drama and not to say anything more about this topic. But her body had a lot to say. During the night, she developed a high fever, so they moved her back to the intensive care unit, where she remained. Her body reacted to the bad news in the letter and promptly the fever came. The opposite of her wishes and hopes came true. Her family became all the more worried. So was her roommate and also her best friend Katy. After three days Isabella was supposed to return to her old room, where she was joyfully welcomed by Annabelle, Thomas, Katy and the meanwhile already so familiar face of her roommate. A few days later, she realized that she had to come to terms with the letter and began to take new courage to face her future. From now on, she could mentally engage in other issues. Everything no longer revolved around Mary's sister's rejection. Isabella gave up on ever meeting Mary's family. She even laughed again. Her roommate was still reading the same romance novel. Isa sat down on the bed with her, even though that was strictly forbidden. "What have you been reading for weeks, anyway?" Curious, she looked at the book cover. "It's a novel about love. Typical for romantic women like me. The writer's name is Ava. She's had countless romance novels out. Don't you know her at all?" the reading-loving roommate explained and asked. Isabella paused and then answered in the negative. She was interested in all literature, but did not know the author or her novels. "Will be done with the novel soon. Would you like to read the book afterwards?" she asked Isabella. "I don't know, get laid off the days. Been here long enough. You're getting laid off too, but we'll keep in touch. Definitely," that was totally important to her. "We stay in touch. Nothing better than that," beamed her neighbor. Neither woman wanted the contact to break off after their hospital stay. They had become far too important and familiar with each other. It was much like with Katy, the humor was omnipresent. That's why she quickly got better. The next morning she unexpectedly received mail ...

Tentatively, the twenty-year-old opened the letter. On the envelope she could find Mary's sister's address. What did it mean? Isabella had not expected another letter. The rejection earlier had been clearly worded, so that even a dreamer like her would understand. She was all the more surprised to receive a letter from Mississippi. Isa tried not to put any expectations into the message. She opened the envelope slowly this time. "If you keep this up, even a snail will open the letter faster than you," her roommate laughed. It wasn't such a long letter this time, but it was going to take a delightful turn. Isabella could hardly believe her luck. She read the short message to the end. "May I ask what it says?" her friend liked to know. "Mary's sister has written again. She continues to want no contact with me. But offers me the address of Mary's best friend and closest confidant. Also from Mississippi. She has already agreed to be in letter contact with me. And funny, her name is also Ava, like your favorite writer." Isabella looked overjoyed. Her roommate was also very happy for her. Then Katy came rushing in, too, and was immediately provided with the latest information. Picking up the phone, Isa called her parents to tell them the good news as well. Jack continued to stay away from the clinic for Isabella's benefit. She already suspected that the relationship did not make sense for her. So she concentrated on getting better. In addition, her current desire played the biggest role. With considerable effort, she wrote a letter to Ava, the best friend of the woman whose heart she had been implanted with. She knew nothing at all about Ava. Only the confirmation and permission to write to her, as well as the postal address from Mississippi. What did one write to a complete stranger? Isabella wanted to try it through Mary. Because both women shared the same fate of being connected to Mary. Isa was so motivated that she wrote all night long. The pages were like a novel in number themselves. She wrote everything off her chest and acted as if she already knew Ava well. And then there was this feeling. Somehow, as she wrote, her heart felt different. Neither right nor wrong, just different. The nurse came into the hospital room in the middle of the night and told Isabella to finally sleep. But she couldn't. Her will was unbroken. The letter should be ready by tomorrow morning at the latest. And it was. A stone fell from her heart when she wrapped the letter and addressed it to Ava. She stuck a stamp on it and then hurried it to the post office. The letter was to go out on time in the morning. Isabella was very happy about the unexpected contact. This letter gave the young patient hope and courage to face life. Her heart was beaming. 'Life can be beautiful and it certainly is. And that, although terrible things also happen here on earth, such as unexpected death', she thought to herself wisely. After taking the letter away to be sent, she and her roommate embraced in deep connection. Knowing they would soon no longer see each other on a daily basis.

All was going to be well, and it was. Isabella spent the rest of her time with her roommate in the hospital. Her blood values were good and her body did not resist the foreign organ. Nevertheless, she found taking the tablets a nuisance, but nevertheless took the medication daily as prescribed. There was a lot of laughter and both women seemed healthier and more relaxed. Isabella looked forward to hearing from Ava soon. Katy and Isabella's parents waited together with her for the reply letter from the still completely unknown woman.

10.

After weeks in the hospital and the vital heart transplant, Isabella was finally allowed home. She was greeted with a colorful, warm welcome hanger. For Isa, walking into the house was like walking into a new life with each step she took. She was given a new life. Thanks to Mary's heart. Isabella seemed happy and grateful to be able to experience it all. She was alive and could look into the eyes of her family and best friend. Katy was also family after all these years. This happiness had been denied to some other patients; she was fully aware of it. Only one wasn't there, and that was her friend Jack. But that didn't throw Isabella off track. She was fine with it, and she wasn't sure if she even wanted to see him? Probably more likely not. There was delicious cake galore to welcome her. Her parents clapped their hands and beamed with joy. Katy was there, too, of course. A family reunion could not have been more beautiful. Fresh flowers were in the living room, in the kitchen, and in her room. Her own room, how terribly she had missed it. Her mother meant very well. She lovingly prepared the house to give her daughter the best possible welcome. The scent of cake, flowers, and lavender cleanser invaded Isabella's nose. Everything in the hospital smelled sterile and not exactly nose-friendly. But the most beautiful thing was the people who surrounded her at home. They were in the hospital every day, too, but seeing them all again at home was like birthday and Christmas together. Love was in the air. And then there were gifts, a pile of gifts. "You're not supposed to get me anything," the former patient was still frugal. "Today it's like celebrating your second birthday this year. You have been given a second life and for that the two of us, your mother and I are infinitely grateful. You have earned the gifts," Thomas explained himself. Totally touched by a photo album and a necklace from her parents, she was given a diary by her best friend. The day couldn't have been better, and in the evening the family ordered Chinese food to celebrate. The first night at home, Isabella slept exceptionally well. Her room was comfortable and furnished as if by that of a young woman. In terms of age, she was in the transitional phase from a teenager to an adult woman, and her room was decorated accordingly. The next day, of course, Katy was visiting again and they watched a hip DVD. It was like old times. The young women chatted and rambled. Then they read each other poems by early 20th century U.S. women poets. Louise Bogan, Dorothy Parker ... inspired the two literary and sports darlings. Uncomfortable things were also part of everyday life. The fact that she could not act like other young people her age continued to be difficult for her. Especially not being able to do so much sports and not being allowed to study at the moment. But luckily there was Katy and her other friends. And fortunately there was also literature that she wanted to discover. Education had continued to be important to her. She wanted to learn, expand her horizons, and distract herself from the physical changes due to the new organ and the pills. The immunosuppressants had their work cut out for them. In the first months after the transplant, the young woman still had to present herself very often for examinations at the clinic. The dosage of the medication was individually adjusted to Isabella. The goal was to stabilize her health and enjoy her new life. As far as that was possible. Isa had to keep a few things in mind so that the transplant would be successful in the long term. Every time she returned from a positive examination at the clinic, the family celebrated with a meal together. Further, she ran to the mailbox daily to see if there was a message from Ava inside. "You don't want her to run like that," Annabelle told her husband as they watched their daughter from the kitchen window. "You'll never get that out of her. She's full of joy. Or have you ever seen a dog that doesn't run toward its master with its tail wagging when he or she comes home from work?" asked Thomas wryly. His wife looked at him in wonder. "What are you talking about? You can't compare that at all. Isabella is not a dog and the unknown Ava is not the master either. I just don't want her to put her health at risk and run like mad to the mailbox." The following Friday there was a little party on life. And Isa was to be the center of attention. Katy discussed everything about the preparations with Isabella's parents in advance. The girlfriends of the twenty-year-old had come. In the evening, the young women threw a pajama party. The girls gave her a book with lots of signatures from other friends addressed to Isabella for her recovery. "Wow, I seem to be really popular," she joked about herself. That was her secret; she never really took herself too seriously. And she didn't care for the talk of others. She kept to herself. Acting like that was quite dangerous at school, because an underdog didn't always have it easy. Her opinion and behavior were usually not aimed at popularity. Then she was also seriously ill and could no longer participate in social life. Despite everything, she had friends and people who missed her. And they were not exactly few. Unfortunately, her roommate from the hospital was not able to come to the pajama party due to her health. Nevertheless, Isabella didn't miss the opportunity to call her the next day and find out how she was feeling. Both women talked and joked on the phone for hours. The connection and familiarity helped both of them in their recovery. The neighbor was not so lucky to be surrounded by so many people in her recovery. That's why contact with Isabella was so important to her. Isa knew how to joke to make her laugh across the phone from her. Laughter still worked wonders. One just had to take advantage of it. And that's what Isabella did for others and, first and foremost, for herself.

With a light exercise program, including yoga and walking, Isabella kept herself fit for the next few weeks. Cognitively, hardly anyone could fool her anyway. Body and mind were not to degenerate. The implanted heart settled well into Isabella's body. Slowly they became one. Mail from Mississippi was still not in the mailbox, but Jack was standing in front of the door. Isabella didn't want to send him away right away, but didn't know how to react to him? He hadn't visited her once since she returned home. The last meeting at the hospital did not go well. She felt pressured and also not comfortable with him just showing up at her door without notice. His visit was therefore cool and distant, without any affection. This time he did not bring a gift, as he usually did. Due to the fact that Isa had almost died recently, she was now free of expectations. This helped her inwardly to slowly close with Jack. After a few hours, he walked back out the door, not bothering to bond with his girlfriend. Isabella was relieved. Once he had been so close to her. He had become stupid, trying to be an adult. That kind of thing didn't go over well with Isabella. She had also changed and evolved. Her values were no longer the same as they had been a few years ago. She noticed that he was not good for her by the fact that she always had to recover after he left. Increasingly, there was nothing positive to be said for the relationship.

On the other hand, the next day was positive. As usual, she ran to the mailbox and this time almost ran into the letter carrier. Grumpy and annoyed, he held a letter in his hand. Thinking she was about to knock him over, he quickly held up his hand, which contained the letter. Full of life as Isabella was, she unexpectedly jumped at the letter carrier and snatched the letter addressed to her from him. They fell together on the floor, which did not interest the young woman. For her, there was only the letter. The man got enormously upset and threatened to press charges. Choleric and upset, he grumbled about the state of his aching back. Slowly he stood up. His bones could be heard cracking loudly. He continued cursing, but then went his way and continued delivering the mail in the neighborhood. Isabella's mother stood behind the kitchen window again. She watched the spectacle and couldn't stop laughing at the choleric letter carrier. The joyful girl pulled open the front door and ran upstairs to her room as fast as she could. "Is it a letter from Ava?", Annabelle asked her daughter. She overheard the question and had disappeared into her room with the mail. The letter was indeed from Ava in Mississippi. Isabella admired the woman's beautiful handwriting. Hardly anyone wrote letters or messages by hand these days. Communication was via smartphones or other devices. Isabella didn't know at the time that Ava was 80 years old. 'Old school,' the recipient of Mary's heart thought to herself. Secretly, Isabella hoped the letter was not a rejection of further writing between her from Louisiana and Ava from Mississippi. Of course, this thought turned out to be pure nonsense. Ava had agreed in advance to written contact. Withdrawing promised was not her way and never lived like that. Isa bravely opened the letter addressed to her and was to be rewarded for her persistent waiting.

A poem of Ava's own writing was in the envelope, along with an invitation to come to Mississippi as soon as Isabella was better. Isa beamed with happiness, reading the invitation carefully. Reading the poem spoke to her heart like never before. No poetry she had ever read triggered this feeling in her. She felt instantly connected to Ava. Not just through the correspondence and the connection to Mary. But rather, the poem felt like it was a part of herself. Her mother stayed downstairs in the house, giving her daughter the space she needed to read the letter alone, which was important to her. Not knowing that enclosed was an invitation for Isabella to visit her neighboring state and a small literary work.

Longing

Longing is the feeling in the search for yourself. Your exterior completely surrounds the vulnerable inner core of your soul. Anchor of your soul say, where are you? Inside you are searching for what you are not able to be. The sea's storm and wind break on you like the waves on the cliffs. The longing of the search for yourself is at the same time the search for your innermost. You creature are pure and perfect with yourself. To bear this requires your highest wise art. If you break on the cliff, you land back in the water to reunite with the waves. If you are ready to go the way again, you start with yourself. If you have found what you were longing for, you have left the longing behind and discovered the joy within you. You are in every smile, in every breath, in the fullness of your gifts and in every answer of your heart.

Moved, Isabella lay on her bed and did not move. She was worried about the poem. And also about Ava, whom she had only known from writing it. 'How can a person be who writes something so emotional? How can a person be who can bring forth such thoughts and turn words into aesthetics? Who is Ava?' Isabella found a new subject, namely her new acquaintance Ava.

In the evening, her father returned from the precinct. Together with his wife, they knocked on their daughter's room door. Overjoyed and stimulated by Ava's written words, she opened the door to her parents. She blurted out that she had received the most beautiful gift in the mail. Isabella gave the contents to her parents to read through themselves. The poem, on the other hand, she read to her parents, who then sat silently and moved with their daughter. Isa was delighted that Mum and Dad felt the same in the beauty of these words as she did. Only what about the invitation to Mississippi? "There is absolutely no question about the respectability of this woman," the policeman said. Annabelle and Thomas looked at each other. "As soon as you're better, you're allowed to drive," the mother directed. "Really, I get to drive?" Isabella threw herself around her parents' necks in joy. "But only when you're feeling better," added the father. Rushing to the phone, Isabella called her friend Katy to tell her about the invitation, the poem, and the upcoming trip.

For the next three months, Isabella did everything she could to make sure her health didn't suffer. She desperately wanted to see Ava, in Mississippi. Meeting Mary's best friend would be the greatest compliment for her and her heart. And apart from that, she already envied Ava, her art of writing poetry. She could hardly wait and therefore did everything possible for her health. At the heart clinic, she continued to be examined extensively. The doctors were amazed at the young woman's good health. What motivation did, it was quite amazing. The states of Mississippi and Louisiana were right next to each other. Yet Isabella had never been there before. That's why she checked the Internet almost daily to see what it looked like there and what could be done locally. What were the people like over there? She was also interested in the bus connection, of course. That was the most important thing she had to deal with for the time being. She also studied the street connections and names of the places. There was enough time to inform herself. She didn't want to start the trip unplanned. And saw it as a great adventure, a new start for her life and a distraction from the daily routine in Louisiana, which was mostly at home. She continued to keep in touch with Ava by letter to keep her informed and to let her know when she would finally be coming. Ava told her in the letters that she was also looking forward to Isabella's visit. That was already a good basis for a relaxed trip.

"Have you thought of everything? And don't forget your medication. Did you bring your passport? You'll also need money, and if you need anything, call anytime. Day or night, anytime. Do you understand?" Isabella rolled her eyes, visibly annoyed. "Yes mum. I've thought of everything. Don't worry so much. Everything will be fine," Isa reassured her mother. "It should be the other way around, don't you think?" joked the father. And then the time had come to say goodbye. While Isabella was in elated excitement due to the trip, her mother could not hide the fact that she already missed her daughter. Thomas was also worried about his only daughter, because the difficult heart transplant was just a few months ago. And personally they did not know Ava yet. They hoped for their intuition and thought positively. Packed and ready to go, they took Isabella to the bus station. Katy was waiting with a Good Travel poster at the bus entrance. "Come back safe and sound," everyone shouted to her. Isabella's mind was on Mississippi by then. "And look at the hotties running around," Katy grinned. Annabelle and Thomas didn't want to hear that and sighed once loudly. "I heard that," Isabella had to laugh and hugged her parents and best friend goodbye. Then she boarded the bus, found her seat and waved to her loved ones from the window. The packed bus started its tour. Isabella continued waving at the window until she could only see her family in the far distance. Isa sat up straight with a smile on her face. The journey and adventure could now begin for her personally. The long-distance bus would take her all the way to Mississippi in a few hours. Listening to music, thinking and reading, she passed the time on the bus until she finally fell asleep.

11.

She was awakened by the bus driver's voice: "Young lady, we are here. You're at your destination." She rubbed her eyes and thanked the attentive driver. "Yes sir, thank you," Isabella picked up her bag and got off. The scent of Mississippi invaded her. Immediately she felt free and relaxed. Ava had hired a man from the neighborhood to pick up the traveler from the bus station and bring her to her home. Isabella was informed about this and was happy to be welcomed for the first time in the neighboring state. During the car ride, she took a good look at the surroundings and the people. How would the first meeting with Mary's best friend go? Curious, Isa let everything come to her. After the drive, they arrived at the idyllic location of Ava's house. Totally charmed by the lovely appearance of her hostess's estate, the young woman got out of the car and thanked Ava's neighbor. Immediately she noticed the colorful, lush flowers that surrounded the house. The fragrance was overwhelming. The neighbor extended many greetings to Ava. He then drove on again. And now she was standing there, at the entrance of the beautiful but still strange house. She was nervous and got a little scared. Awe at the situation came through to her. Isabella stood in front of the white facade of the house as if ordered and not picked up. She didn't dare to just walk in. Having survived the heart transplant well and having already been through a lot, there was really nothing left to be afraid of. The birds were chirping, she watched an airplane fly overhead in the sky. As soon as she looked at the house again, she wanted to enter it. But she couldn't. She still stood there, nervous and with her mouth slightly open. The short while seemed like minutes to her. Suddenly someone opened the door. As if rooted to the spot, Isa stood there and did not move. Who was coming out now? What happened was what she had not expected. An older, chic lady stood in the doorway and moved a step toward the porch. 'Who is that?" the young woman thought to herself. As if she had said it out loud, she greeted her opposite with, 'Good afternoon. You must be Isabella? Did you have a good journey?" Isa's breath caught in her throat. Surely this could never be Ava? A white, old woman. This was not how she had imagined Mary's best friend. 'It can't be?" she repeated in her mind. Stuttering slowly, she replied, "Yes, I'm Isabella. How do you do?" Ava approached her and extended her hand in greeting. Isabella returned the formal handshake. The moment their two hands touched, it hit Isabella like a lightning bolt. A very strange feeling permeated her body. She did not dare to ask if the lady could be Ava? The certainty was taken from her: "Oh, excuse me. I haven't even introduced myself yet. I am Ava. We've been writing letters, and I'm Mary's best friend." Isabella would have liked to sink into the ground. How she should react now, she didn't know. She still didn't realize why she was so puzzled. Maybe because Ava was white and old? Hadn't she expected that?

Isabella's father was dark-skinned and her mother half white and half black. They belonged together like the sun and the moon. Thus, Isa was blessed by everything her family was able to give. Did Isabella have prejudices? She knew that Mary was 40 years old before she died and that she must have been a dark-skinned, strong woman. It made sense to Isa to assume that Mary's best friend was also dark-skinned and about the same age as the once-deceased. But things turned out differently. Isabella wanted to find out why Mary and Ava had been such close confidants? She thus had a job to do in Mississippi. "Do you like to come in? Standing here all this time must be boring for you?", Ava went ahead into the house. Shyly and slowly, she followed the older lady. "This is my house. I'll show you to your room now. You're welcome to freshen up in the bathroom if you like. Surely you still have to let your parents know that you arrived safely?", Ava acted very hospitable and thought along. Together they walked up the slightly creaky wooden stairs in the imposing, fine house. The room had been nicely prepared by Ava for Isabella beforehand. Japanese anemone and white lilac stood in a hand-embellished flower vase. The white bedding was decorated with playful ruffles. A rose-colored, hand-knotted rug lay on the hardwood floor. A pitcher of fresh water along with a French drinking glass stood on a wooden sideboard. The closet was also carved from old dark wood and could have brought a smile to the face of any carpenter. The fresh scent of Ava's garden drifted in through the half-open window. "If you need anything else, let me know. I'll be downstairs," she informed Isabella. The latter thanked her and began to enjoy the beauty of the decor in the room before calling her parents and Katy. Afterwards, she disappeared briefly into the bathroom to change into new clothes after the long journey. Dried lavender hung scattered from the ceiling in the bathroom, which was decorated in art nouveau style. It was as if time had stood still in this house. But in a charming, chic and stylish way. At home in Louisiana, it was also cozy, yet furnished in a more modern and contemporary way. Here it was not old-fashioned, nor unfashionable, but like fine gentlemen. Somehow Isabella liked that, and yet she was shy to start a conversation with the older lady. Ava made an educated and intelligent impression on Isa. Despite her age, she seemed to have remained cosmopolitan. And she could convince herself of her literary abilities in the poem Longing. Fear of breaking something remained with every movement. Accordingly, she crept quietly and slowly down the stairs, which was not to go unnoticed. "You don't have to be extra quiet. It's been quiet enough here since Mary died." Isabella cringed and immediately apologized. She wanted to do everything right, but it wasn't. A little more relaxed, she walked down the rest of the steps normally. "You wrote that you like

Chinese food. That's why I ordered us some. China Garden are the best supplier from the area," Ava informed her guest. Isabella was getting more and more nervous. The hostess seemed so perfect to her, so controlled and slightly distant. How was the ice ever going to be broken between them? "You shouldn't have," the twenty-year-old stammered. The silence after that was interrupted by the ringing of the deliveryman. 'Phew, thank goodness,' Isabella was relieved. She puffed her lips and made her way to the living room, then to the kitchen. The kitchen was also as old, but extremely chic as its owner. Fresh fruit and yellow lemons lay arranged on a clay bowl. The young woman's mouth almost watered at the sight of the rest of the kitchen supplies. Healthy vegetables stood in open wooden crates on the cool floor, pasta was decoratively stowed in a glass container, and vanilla beans from Mexico were to be used for baking. Isabella almost looked her fill. Ava set the dining table in the living and dining room with old, white-blue china. Golden cutlery made the impression perfect. "Isn't, this way too fine for Chinese out of the paper container?" Isa gradually began to open up. Questioning and incomprehensible, Ava looked at the young woman and confidently replied, "Child remember this. A little elegance in everyday life makes life more beautiful." The way she expressed herself, so was her lifestyle. The food from the Chinese delivery service tasted exquisite to Isabella. The trip had made her hungry. Everywhere outside and inside the house smelled of fresh flowers, vanilla and lavender. "With Mary, I occasionally drank a good drop of fine red wine. Because of your age and illness, I'll spare you as well as myself. Tonight I'll leave it at a glass of water," Ava reminisced. The evening went by still a bit restrained and lacking in communication. A little embarrassed, Isabella thanked them for their hospitality and the meal, before retiring to her room. Once again, she called her parents. "Honey, you don't have to stay if you don't want to. No one is forcing you. It's great that the woman is nice and polite, but if she's too old for you and you can't connect with her, you can always come home," Mama advised Annabelle. "Thanks mum. I'll think about it. Have a good evening you and dad. Love you," and hung up. Unexpectedly, Isabella slept well the first night in her guest bed. The next morning she stretched and stretched, starting to make her way to the bathroom as the scent of freshly brewed coffee and jam hit her nose. "Good morning," the two women greeted each other. After breakfast, the sunbathers gravitated to the porch of the house. Ava did not talk about herself directly, but at length about Mary, Isabella's organ donor. Curious and interested, the operated listened to everything. There was no doubt that Mary had the heart Isabella had always wanted as a recipient. The ice was broken and Isa even asked questions about her lifesaver. She wanted to know everything about Mary. Time passed frantically. Isabella also told parts of her life story to Ava, who also listened attentively and eagerly. What Isa didn't notice, however, was that the older lady only talked about Mary and the common bond but not about herself. Unnoticed, Isabella thanked Mary's best friend for her donation. She also wanted to tell Mary's sister, but she had wanted to avoid contact. And because Isabella was just beginning to thank her for everything, she brought up Ava's wonderful poem Longing and how much it touched her at this stage. After the women sat and philosophized on the porch for most of the day, Isabella followed up with a quiet look around her hostess's big, beautiful house and discovered lots of little treasures and photos of Mary.

Word of Isabella's visit from Louisiana had already spread through the town of Ava. Such information spread as fast as fire. This had also reached Mary's sister and her family. As a result, an argument raged at their home. "Mother, she didn't do anything to you or us. And it's not her fault that Mary died. I just want to meet her. Please let me go to Ava," Benji asked his mother. She was raging with anger and couldn't control herself. She screamed so loudly that half the neighborhood could hear. "No Benjamin. You will not go. And I forbid you to meet her," the mother let her temper run wild. "So what if I do go? You can't stop me. I'm not a child anymore, I'm 25 years old. Mary was my aunt and I want to see in whose heart she lives on," Benji was sure of his request. His mother reacted completely indignant, heated and extremely sensitive to this issue. "I can't believe you would betray our family. Don't I mean anything to you?" the mother felt personally hurt. Benjamin's father and Mary's brother-in-law was caught between two stools. He didn't know how to act and what seemed right? "Why don't you calm down? Arguing doesn't do anyone any good. We've already lost Mary. I don't want to lose you guys to something like this, too," he got off his chest. It was quiet for a moment, but the silence didn't last long. Benji did not hesitate and acted immediately. Hastily he took his backpack and disappeared through the door to meet Isabella. Since it was already evening and he by no means wanted to show up so upset at Ava and the unknown recipient of Mary's heart, Benjamin wandered the streets and spent half the night in a snack bar. The next morning, Isa and her hostess visited Mary's grave. Since Ava's garden was bursting with flowers, they picked the most beautiful bouquet for their sweetheart and brought it to the grave. "Here she lies. This is the woman who lent you her heart," Ava stood with Isabella in front of Mary's final resting place. Isa spoke aloud to the deceased, "Hello Mary. It's me, Isabella. I wanted to say hello to you and most of all thank you for letting me carry your heart inside me. It's nice to meet you through Ava. She has already told me a lot about you. And I've been looking at your photos. They're beautiful." Composed, both women stood in front of the grave, getting really close for the first time since Isabella's arrival. The first step came from the twenty-year-old; she took Ava in her arms. Delighted at this, the octogenarian returned the hug. They stood with Mary for a while longer, placing the flowers on the gravestone and talking about the deceased. "It's so warm, feel like a bittersweet lemonade?", expectantly Ava looked at Isabella. "Well, I'm in. It's good to go from me." Both women left the gravesite, secretly glad to have grown emotionally closer. Once home, the old lady went to her kitchen to prepare the lemonade and slice the yellow lemons. Isabella sat on the porch steps enjoying the beautiful Mississippi weather and the natural scent of the flowers. Suddenly and completely unexpectedly, a young man approached the house. To Isabella, it made the impression of matter-of-factness as the young man walked toward Ava's house. "Hi. You must be the guest from Louisiana. I'm Benjamin, but everyone calls me Benji. I'm Mary's nephew," he said as he held out his hand to Isabella in greeting. 'Wow. Mary's nephew looks great and seems so nice' Isabella was instantly delighted. "Hello Benji. My name is Isabella and that's right; I'm the guest from Louisiana. Nice to meet you," Isa noticed her heart was beating faster than it had been a few minutes ago. She liked Benjamin and hopefully he would stay? Ava came outside without the lemonade and was excited to see Benjamin. "Ava," the young man called out, running into her arms. "I'm so glad you're here. I'm so happy to see you. But surely your parents didn't let you do that?" Ava realized this immediately. She had a lot of life experience, there was no fooling her anymore. She already suspected that Benji would be here without his mother's permission. Feeling caught, he said, "You always know everything, too. But that's okay. I'm 25 years old and I can make my own decisions. Luckily." At that, he looked at Isabella. Ava immediately noticed the sympathy between the two young adults. "Well, then, you must have met Isabella? She's the young woman who had your aunt's heart implanted," Ava said. Somewhat sheepishly, Benjamin replied that he had just met Isabella. "Well, I'll get out three glasses of lemonade now," Ava grinned, leaving the two young people to themselves for a moment. With fresh, homemade lemonade, the three celebrated their friend Mary and Isabella's new life a short time later, as she continued to live through Mary's heart. Benjamin made himself directly useful and guided the plug of the lantern light chain into the socket. Just as colorful as Ava's flowers in the garden, the lights shone in all colors. Isabella's own first action as a visitor to Mississippi was to light the candles on the porch. A beautiful atmosphere was created. The three of them chatted harmoniously and had to laugh at one or two of Mary's jokes. Ava and Benji had saved everything about their friend and aunt as a memory. For the first time, happiness entered the house again, which was in danger of dying after the death of Mary herself. The boisterous mood also attracted people from the neighborhood, who came to Ava's house again after a long time. The hostess introduced all the neighbors and friends to Isabella. These were the southern states. Sudden unexpected visit with unplanned celebration. There was talk, sometimes loud, sometimes a little louder, and lots of laughter. And of course a lot of eating and drinking. Isa met so many new people that she and Benjamin had no time to talk alone. The day and evening passed quickly. After everyone present had helped clean up, Isabella thanked Ava for the beautiful day and retired to her room. But first she said goodbye to her new acquaintance, young Benji. He did not want to miss the opportunity to tell Isabella that he would certainly come back tomorrow. Once in her room, she looked at her cell phone, which showed ten missed calls. Immediately Isa rang her mother. "We were already worried. Why didn't you call us back? Your father and I wanted to know how you were? You were thinking about possibly going home," a worried Annabelle spoke to her daughter on the phone. Isabella quickly gave the all-clear and told about the great day she had today. Of the visit to Mary's grave, the delicious lemonade, the thoughtful hospitality of Ava, the little party on the porch with the neighbors, and, of course, Benjamin. "Oh, you met someone?", for Thomas no man could be good enough for his daughter. He saw for himself that the relationship with Jack, his daughter with heart disease, was no longer good. "No dad. He's Mary's nephew and just wanted to introduce himself. But he's nice," Isa grinned through the cell phone. Beaming with joy, Isabella finished talking to her parents. "Well, this is going to be fun. Having just undergone surgery, our little one is already traveling and meeting new Benjamins," Thomas told his wife. She immediately noticed the jealousy her husband felt. "He just wanted to introduce himself. That's how it usually starts," grumbled the father. "I think you need a little distraction. How about a relaxing massage and a good glass of wine to go with it?" Annabelle looked deep into her husband's eyes. He couldn't resist the tempting offer and fetched two wine glasses from the cabinet. Meanwhile, sleep was still out of Isabella's mind. She only had Benji on her mind and hoped to actually see him again tomorrow. Full of happy hormones in her body, she rang her best friend Katy at the end of the day to tell her about the day and, first and foremost, about meeting Mary's 25-year-old nephew. Afterwards, Isa lay in bed with her eyes open and couldn't fall asleep. At some point, she tired out and fell asleep, shallow and reassured.

Benjamin kept his promise and came back to visit Ava and Isabella the next day. Since the weekend started that day, Benji had no other obligations. Isabella was looking at Ava's library at the same time, fascinated, and was suddenly disturbed by a loud noise. She was startled and stopped. Her heart and body were still finely attuned to loud noises. Where was this ghastly sound coming from? She followed her auditory perception and opened the front door. It was Benji, mowing the lawn for Ava. "Good afternoon dear Isabella," he greeted her and stopped the lawn mower. At the sight of Mary's nephew, Isabella's eyes sparkled with joy. "Hi Benji. Great that you're helping her," Isa threw compliments at her crush.

"Before my aunt died in that terrible accident, I was here every day. Well, that's how it can come. Where's Ava?" The old lady was like family to him, so he worried about the octogenarian. "She's in her writing room. She said she had to do something," Isa replied with a dreamy look. Benjamin thought about it for a moment and suggested a great idea to his guest: "Hey, tell me Isabella. Do you have any plans for today? If Ava is in her writing room, then you and I could do something. If you want to? Besides the cemetery, I'm sure you haven't seen much of Mississippi?" Isabella could hardly believe her luck. Of course she wanted to do something with him. She tried to play it cool, babbling something like, "I'll have to think about it, but I think I already have time." Isa still wanted to come across as aloof and cool. "Fine," Benjamin said, and continued mowing the lawn. Isabella didn't want to just leave right away, so she informed Ava about the trip. The old lady's office door was open a crack, so Isabella could just peek through it. Ava sat in her chair and bent her forearm on the desk. Again and again she shook her head, as if something was wrong. She looked thoughtful and didn't write a single word. Isa was embarrassed to knock in this situation, she didn't want to disturb. A sign to make herself noticed was the clearing of throat from her mouth. Ava was startled by this and immediately turned around. Isabella was so uncomfortable to have disturbed the educated lady while she was thinking that she turned around and wanted to leave. "What's the matter? Don't you like the library?", Ava didn't know how to ask anything else. "No, no, it's all good. The library is wonderful. I was just wondering if I could go on a field trip with Benjamin later? He wanted to show me around," Isa looked at her hostess with expectant eyes. She wished them both a lot of fun and a nice day. Motivated, Isa went to her guest room to pick out a suitable outfit for the upcoming excursion. Apart from jeans and T-shirts, she didn't have much with her. Isabella was no fashionista, she had her own taste. Quickly grabbing her cell phone, she called Katy to get a tip on which of her many t-shirts she could wear? She felt as if she had a date today. Accordingly, she was excited, knowing that it was going to be a harmless meeting and that she didn't even know Benjamin very well. An hour later, the two met down the hall. "Are you ready to go? I've got something great in mind," Benji was good at planning. "I'm ready," she beamed at Benjamin. They said goodbye to Ava and started their trip together. "Are you up for nature?" the nephew of Mary asked his new acquaintance from Louisiana. "And how. My illness kept me confined to the hospital for weeks and then home. That's why I was so looking forward to visiting Mississippi. To learn all about Mary, of course. But also to get out, move around, and meet people. I loved sports so much back then." Isabella babbled without thinking. "Well, then this trip is just what you need," Benji was sure. He had planned a trip to Bienville national Forest. But he didn't tell Isa about it yet. A bus was to take them there. Excited to see what Benjamin came up with, she settled in for the bus ride. There were tourists sitting there, just like herself, who wanted to see the area. During the ride, the two talked as if they were longtime friends. With eye contact and a smile, they would soon arrive at the forest. Impressed by the beauty of nature, the two got off the bus and looked at the surroundings. Like two hikers, they strolled through the Forest. The green of the trees indicated the health of the forest. The fresh smell of nature made the day even more pleasant and almost perfect. And Benjamin played the guide: "Welcome to the Bienville national Forest. I hope madame likes it here? The 723 square kilometer area was established in 1934 by buying the forests directly from local logging companies. It was named after Jean-Baptiste le Moyne de Bienville." Isabella was so enraptured that she could not follow Benjamin's words, but only looked into his eyes. At the tourist information office, the two borrowed two bicycles and explored the peaceful forest by bike. Isabella had not felt as good as she did that day for a long time. She liked Benjamin very much, and this was mutual. After all, he had jeopardized his relationship with his parents just to get to know Isa. The twenty-year-old's operated body didn't mind the bike ride at all, quite the opposite. She felt free and carefree. In the forest, there were lakes and rivers to relax by, in addition to various recreational and leisure activities. The two parked their bikes at a lake and lay down on a borrowed blanket. As if they were longtime confidants, the young woman settled into

Benjamin's arm. At that moment, there could be nothing better than to enjoy and be silent. The forest with its pines and oaks was known for its abundance of birds. Over 170 different species of birds lived in this forest. "I feel like I could stay here forever. Don't you?" she asked her flock, hoping he would feel the same. And he obviously felt the same: "You, the trees and the birds chirping ... I'm impressed," he replied. Whatever he was impressed by, Isabella felt connected to him. The day could have gone on forever, but before it got dark, they should have left the forest as a day tourist. Isabella felt as if she had been reborn. They got on the bikes and rode back to the tourist information. Handing in both bikes and the blanket, they walked back to the bus stop, refreshed. During the bus ride, Isa leaned on her newfound friend. She felt guilty toward Jack, but she hadn't had such a nice day with him in a long time. In fact, she seemed certain that she had never felt as comfortable with anyone as she did with Benjamin. But she didn't know that before, because she only got to know this feeling through Benji. Back at the house, Ava could see the two of them caring for each other. She had prepared a delicious dinner and invited the two young people to dinner. "Thank you Ava. But I have to get home before Mum freaks out even more. Thanks for everything. And Isabella, it was a wonderful day," Benji said goodbye to the ladies. "Thank you to you, too. I will never forget the day. And come home safe," Isabella's interest in Benjamin grew more and more that she didn't even want to go back home. She felt completely comfortable and healthy in the state of Mississippi.

The next few days she helped out a lot around the house. Isa cleaned, swept, vacuumed and ironed. She wanted to help Ava and thus thank her for her thoughtful hospitality. Apart from that, the housework was a good distraction from the thought of having to go home again soon. The exercise was good for her and her body. Her hostess was 80 years old, and Isabella was tremendously ashamed if she didn't help enough. Ava was not ready for a new housekeeper. The loss of Mary sat deep within her and would not go away anytime soon. Mary was not only the best housekeeper, but also a contact person, confidant and best friend. Letting a stranger into the house was something she couldn't do yet. With Isabella it was different. She carried Mary's heart inside her and seemed worthy of it. Isa understood the octogenarian on this point. Mary had been in and out of her home for so many years, she lived there in feeling as well. The trust was never in question. Ava had to digest her friend's death first. Isabella thought how nice it would be to stay for longer and help her hostess. Of course also to get to know Benjamin further. Of course, he came to visit again. The quarrel with his mother was still not settled, but he could make decisions on his own at the age of 25. He felt drawn to his new acquaintance; a warmth surrounded him every time he saw Isabella. The trip to Bienville national Forest brought the two closer together. Benji liked her and wanted to get to know the young lady from Louisiana further. And Ava was a very special subject to Benjamin anyway. She was his late aunt's best friend. Even before Isabella arrived, he had been visiting the old lady in Mississippi almost daily at her home. The way Mary and Ava interacted and the harmony in the house always attracted him. He was also impressed that Ava worked as a writer and had an all-encompassing knowledge. He often felt inspired and learned a lot. He never wanted to end up like the gangsters and groups out there on the streets. Young, black men in particular often got caught up in such criminal systems and structures. He realized that the house of Ava saved him from that. His goal was to become a good person. Perhaps he already was? Aunt Mary always saw the best in him.

It had not escaped Isabella's notice that Ava wrote romance novels. And from what she heard, quite successfully. She had already published 50 books in her lifetime. The twenty-year-old was always amazed at how Ava was still working hard at the age of 80. Be it at her desk, in the garden or around the house. Her way of speaking indicated an educated status. She was worth listening to. The writer did not offer her novels to anyone. It was Isabella who asked if she could read a romance novel of hers? It was okay for her hostess, millions of fans around the world gave their approval to the works years ago. Ava never cared about prizes and awards. She never imagined anything about it. This impressed Isabella and also Benjamin independently even more. "She is a world star and never got a high ...," Isabella read in an old newspaper article about the intellectual lady. 'What a role model.' Isa dived into the romance novel. She spent an entire week immersed in a written love story by Ava, helping around the house, exchanging ideas with Ava about her novels and inventions, and seeing Benji. He was present in the same house every day anyway. He helped the old lady in the garden. Isabella sat either in the library, in the living room or on the porch to indulge in the passionate novel. The day was coming to say goodbye. 'It's hard to believe my time in Mississippi is already up. If only I could stay here,' Isabella thought wistfully to herself. Her health was better than ever. The lady of the house lovingly packed her provisions for the long bus trip. She took the novel home with her so that she could continue to read it and study it in depth in Louisiana. Isabella once again walked through the beautiful house with full mindfulness and was inwardly filled with gratitude for the beautiful moments. She met Ava and Benji, whom she had never heard of a year ago. The most important thing, the visit to Mary's grave, meant everything to her. From the trip to the woods with Benjamin, she knew what it meant in the beginning to feel comfortable and safe with someone. The trip to Mississippi made her learn a few things in life. Her wealth of experience was broadened. When would she see them again? One thing was clear, she carried them both with her in her heart to Louisiana. The acquaintance from the neighborhood, who had already brought Isabella from the bus station to Ava, was to play cab again. The octogenarian placed herself on the passenger seat, Isa and Benji sat in the back. As if they were keeping a little secret, the two held hands during the car ride. Benjamin found it difficult to let go of his new acquaintance, who meant a lot to him. Hesitantly, he got out of the car after the ride. The two young people had tears in their eyes as they watched the bus to Louisiana pull up in front of them. Ava also found it hard to say goodbye. She just found it easier not to let it show. She was already fond of the young visitor, and not just because she carried Mary's heart. She placed a wreath of flowers she had tied herself on Isabella's hair. "How beautiful. I love your colorful flowers from the garden. Ava, thank you so much for everything. And I want to see you again, too," Isa was serious. The two women embraced each other intimately. Ava knew this affection only from the friendship between her and Mary. The usually rather aloof Ava did not hug anyone just so intimately. It was Isabella who dared to make the first move. Ava was extremely grateful to her for that. Then it was Benji's turn. "I want to see you again, too. Whether it's in Mississippi or Louisiana. And I want to get to know you further," Benjamin could not have expressed himself better. With that, he returned Isabella's feelings. With painful partings, the two accepted the physical separation for a while. Just as Isabella was about to board the bus, an unknown woman came running up, calling her. Isa turned around startled and knew nothing to say. "Mum, Dad, what are you doing here?" asked Benjamin to his parents who had just arrived. "Isabella, I'm sorry I didn't want any contact with you and also forbade my son to visit Ava in the house. I just couldn't help it. I am the sister of Mary, the woman whose heart you carry under your chest. Please forgive me. Benjamin likes you and if you are the one who got my sister's heart, you shall be welcome in my family. Even if my words come a little late," Benjamin's mother spoke ruefully. The happy ending in Mississippi was perfect. The young visitor hugged Benjamin's parents and forgave them for their rejection before boarding the bus for the return trip to Louisiana. "We'll talk on the phone," the two young hearts decided. She found friends in Mississippi and certainty as to whom her heart came from. All four waved after the departing bus. Ava's neighbor and driver waited patiently in the parking lot to take Ava back home. Unfortunately, without Isabella, who drove home with one laughing eye and one crying eye. Benji got into the car with his parents. The fight over Isabella was forgiven and forgotten. And somehow, Benjamin's parents liked the fun-loving and friendly Isabella right away.

12.

The vacationer was welcomed in Louisiana with waving flags. Her parents and Katy stood at the bus stop and welcomed their bestie. "Honey, it's so good to see you and to know that you had a good time after all. You look good," Annabelle hugged her daughter tightly. Her father Thomas stroked her hair and admired the creative flower arrangement on her head. "Finally. We have her back," he couldn't help himself. "You have to tell me all about this Benji. I can't wait," Katy was back in her element. The family got in the car and headed home. To celebrate, they had Chinese food as usual. "You guys should try the Chinese place in Ava's neighborhood. I'm telling you. It's a taste explosion," the homegirl raved. "So you've been doing well? You seem really happy and refreshed," her dad noticed. Isa couldn't deny that. She would have preferred to say that Benjamin's getting to know her was related to her well-being. But she didn't want to make her father unnecessarily jealous. "And what about Jack? Have you seen him or heard from him?", Isa wanted to know and distract. She wasn't really interested in Jack anymore, but he was still her steady boyfriend. Embarrassed, all three looked to the floor. "He was here and wanted to know where you were and why you weren't answering your cell phone? After he rang here three times, we told him you were in Mississippi visiting. To meet your heart donor's best friend there," the mother explained. "And then?" wanted to know Isabella. "Nothing more. He kept silent and immediately went out the door. From then on we didn't see him again," Annabelle continued "Why didn't you tell him the truth?" Thomas didn't understand. Isabella looked thoughtful and answered with conviction that her friend would not have understood. "He's changed and he's not the cool, laid back Jack he used to be. He wants to know everything and doesn't share my opinion anymore," Isa added honestly. "It just shows that the boy is interested in you when he wants to know something. He was here asking about you too. If Jack didn't like you, he wouldn't have come," Thomas saw on Jack's part the interest in his daughter. Isabella had long since realized that she no longer felt comfortable with Jack, but she did with Benjamin. She still kept this to herself. She wanted to keep a little secret from Mississippi.

On the very second day in Louisiana, Isabella had to go to the clinic where her heart was transplanted for an examination. The examinations lasted all day. "Your values are all good and you make a vital impression. That's not the case after every heart transplant," the senior physician basically only confirmed how Isabella really felt. "Keep taking care of yourself, take it easy and take your pills every day," that's all the doctor had to say. What struck Isa was that the doctor spoke only of the medical aspect. But much more, and Isabella was sure of this, a significant part of the visit to Mississippi contributed to her recovery. And the joy it brought to her life. "Scientific medicine is life support, but love and joy are in the heart, the juice you take while you are using medicine." These words actually came out of Isabella. The attending's reaction to this was an open mouth. "Love and joy, yes," he shook his head thoughtfully and disappeared into the next treatment room. Isabella's parents understood by now what their daughter was trying to say. The blood results were good and Isa hadn't looked so fresh, healthy and recovered in a long time. "It obviously wasn't a mistake to have her travel to Mississippi. Something must have happened there to make her so positive," Thomas thought for a moment, but was more pleased with his daughter's health. That evening, Isabella made herself comfortable on her bed at home. Curious, she wondered how Ava's romance novel would continue? Annabelle brought her daughter upstairs hot chocolate with soft marshmallows. Into the night, Isa hung over the book and immersed herself in Ava's penned love story.

The next noon was going to be a busy one. Jack came to visit unexpectedly. He rang the front doorbell and was kindly invited in by Annabelle. Even as the doorbell rang, Isabella startled and immediately got a bad feeling. Her heart was pounding too fast, it shouldn't be. With each step Jack hurried up, Isabella felt worse. Her breathing became uncontrolled and she began to sweat. "Hey, there you are," Jack stood in the doorway with his mischievous smile. "Hi Jack.

Yes, here I am again," Isabella answered quietly. He walked up to his girlfriend to greet her with a kiss on the mouth. Quickly, the perky young woman replied that a kiss on the mouth was still too dangerous and not to stand in the way of recovery. She already knew how to escape Jack's physical closeness and attention. He seemed anything but happy about it and pulled an annoyed face. Immediately and without any ado, he brought up Isabella's trip to Mississippi. "Why didn't you tell me you were leaving our state and taking a bus trip to Mississippi? Just to meet your heart donor's girlfriend. That is completely irresponsible to your health. I have never heard of anyone going on vacation after a heart transplant. And you go alone to a complete stranger and don't even tell your own friend. What the hell are you thinking? And then you don't even want to kiss me as a greeting because it's too dangerous for you. But take a long trip, you can!" Jack threw accusations at his girlfriend, trying to trigger a guilty conscience in her. Everything he said sounded Contra Isabella. His angry and patronizing manner made Isa move away from him even more. She pretended to be combative and didn't want to give any space to his anger. And she wasn't going to let it all go to waste. "At the hospital, you already didn't want to understand me. You don't support me in my plans and get upset when I have my own ideas and act accordingly. You would never have let me leave Louisiana on my own. And by the way ... Ava has not just been a friend of Mary's. The connection went deeper and everyone can learn from that. Through our correspondence, I was able to get to know her in advance, and I didn't leave immediately after the surgery. I was not irresponsible either, because my blood values are good and I am better than ever. The senior physician said so himself," the young woman argued confidently, almost aggressively. Her body, on the other hand, found this argument more difficult from sentence to sentence. The former discussion in the hospital and the argument about the visit to Mississippi came to a sad end. Jack left Isabella just like that and went out the door once again. Isa was left in her room with wet, sweaty clothes. Her mother came upstairs and was most concerned about her only daughter. Isabella was lying on the bed, panting and throbbing. Damp compresses Annabelle put on her beloved and secretly prayed alongside. It took the whole evening for Isa to calm down physically. Later, she lay downstairs on the living room couch with her parents. Together they watched a program on TV. Katy, of course, also came to check on her best friend. The following night, Isabella slept fitfully. Her body felt as morbid as it did before the surgery. Katy had stayed the night to sleep next to her friend and to check on her. One room over, the heart patient's parents were tremendously worried about their daughter. "When she came back from Mississippi, she looked so refreshed and almost healthy. Her voice sounded happy, she was at peace with herself. Learning who she had the heart of did her good. So did the contact with Ava and Benjamin," Annabelle summarized. The parents looked at each other sadly. The mother had so much on her mind that she wanted to say and that upset her. "Jack has always been a good friend to our daughter. He stood by her and visited her in the hospital. All the gifts and attention. And now what? The fact is, when Jack and Isabella run into each other, she's not doing well. In fact, lately, she's been pretty bad. And our daughter has a disease, I don't want to lose her to trouble with Jack. Not after she's come through the heart transplant well and she's been doing great in Mississippi." The couple felt powerless in the situation. They wanted to help Isabella, to allow her to continue to live a life in recovery. They were all the more surprised to watch the longtime couple part ways. "God will stand by us and especially our daughter," Thomas sought divine assistance. Together, the couple prayed that all would be well.

A bad night was followed by a good morning. Annabelle prepared a powerful breakfast for her daughter and his best friend. Healing glad that her daughter had made it through the night, she gave her a big kiss on the forehead. "I'd like to go to the heart clinic with you today. After Jack's visit yesterday and your poor condition, your father and I think it's appropriate to have you checked out today," the mother beast in Annabelle came out. Isabella realized on her own what the argument with Jack brought out in her. She was even a little annoyed, because the argument and the excitement would not have been necessary. Before Jack's visit, she was happy. And now she was miserable again. Responsibly, Isabella agreed to an examination at the clinic. Her mother had already made an appointment with the senior physician that morning. A contact person was available at all times for urgent emergencies involving patients who had undergone surgery. Katy accompanied mother and daughter to the clinic. Once again, the young patient was thoroughly examined and checked. "That went well again. But you should continue to take it easy. By that I mean avoid any trouble. Even if it means you have to break off contact," the senior physician spoke plainly. Isa had understood what the doctor was trying to say. Relieved, the three women drove back home.

Isabella spent the next week continuing to read Ava's 500-page novel and staying in correspondence with the writer about it. Isa also informed the octogenarian about private matters from Louisiana. About the fight with Jack and the subsequent examination in the hospital. Of course, Ava wrote letters back to her much younger friend in her most beautiful handwriting. Isabella also telephoned her former roommate from the hospital to exchange ideas, cheer each other up and give strength. Her physical and mental condition got a little better. Isa went walking every day and was visited by friends. Among them was Katy, of course, who seemed to have almost moved in with Isabella's family. The longing for

Mississippi grew steadily in Isabella's heart. There were the conversations with Ava, her beautiful house, and not to forget - Benjamin. She wanted to see him and spend time with him, every day she had to think about him.

With her mother, the twenty-year-old went to the local supermarket to get groceries, washing powder and other things from the shopping list. Here they usually met friends or acquaintances with whom they had short or long conversations. The visit to the huge supermarket never lasted less than an hour. The family usually bought so much there that they needed two shopping carts. Annabelle held her list and pushed one cart in front of her. Isabella carried the second list and grabbed a blue shopping cart as well. Between daydreaming and shopping lists, Isa strolled through the endless expanse of supermarket aisles. Until, all of a sudden, her cell phone rang. Just as she could tell from the front doorbell that Jack was the visitor, this time she sensed it was Benjamin calling. The feeling was right. His number was on her display that she almost dropped to the floor with euphoria. Excited, but seeming totally cool, she answered her cell phone. In an excited voice, she said, "Benji. Hi, how are you?" She almost drove the blue shopping cart into a shelf. The sweet, friendly and interested voice of Benjamin from Mississippi sent hundreds of butterflies flying through Isabella's stomach. She felt like she was in paradise and on cloud nine at the same time, and only because she heard Benjamin's voice. She no longer noticed the people around her. The shopping list was forgotten and the flirtation on the phone was initiated. She felt alive. Shopping turned into phone dating, which brought hearts to the young woman's eyes. Hearing his voice felt like feeling the most beautiful thing in the world. Yet she didn't see or touch Benjamin at all. Only his voice gave her peace and confidence. But the short-lived peace was to be disturbed again. While Isabella was flirting with 25-year-old Benji on her cell phone, a guest at the supermarket secretly overheard. Isa was overheard and observed without noticing. She was too engrossed in the phone conversation. 'I don't believe it. She has someone else ... ', thought a bystander. It was Jack, who happened to be shopping at the supermarket at the same time as Isabella and her mother. He was going to get soft drinks and thought he recognized the voice from the side aisle. Inconspicuously, he looked between the boxes and recognized his girlfriend, who was apparently having an amusing conversation with another man on her cell phone. Jealously, he surprised his girlfriend in her hallway, who almost dropped her cell phone in shock. Jack felt betrayed and lied to. He did not want to let this happen to him. The young woman's heart was pounding at that moment not because of the butterflies in her stomach, but because of fear of Jack's reaction to her phone call. "That's what I thought. You have someone else and you're cheating on me. And after all I've done for you," the angry man's voice spoke up. "Isabella, who is this? Do you need help? Please say something!", Benjamin spoke in concern to Isabella through his cell phone. "I have to hang up. I'll call you later," pushing the call away. "No Jack. This is complete bullshit. I don't have anyone else and I've never cheated on you," Isa immediately justified herself. "And who was that on the phone? You could hear your flirting all the way to Acapulco," Jack raised his voice. "That's just a friend. Someone I met in Mississippi. And of course Jack, thank you for everything you've done for me," Isabella tried to remain firm. Annabelle had never lost her maternal instinct. Going to check on her daughter, she spotted Isabella and Jack in aisle number ten. She immediately noticed the renewed argument between the two and spoke up for her ailing daughter. "Hello Jack. What are you getting so loud about?" He was at a loss for words in response. He would rather settle this with his girlfriend alone. But Annabelle stood protectively in front of her only and beloved daughter. "Isabella, is there anything else you want to say to Jack? Otherwise, I suggest we pay and then go!" Her mother's suggestion came at the right time. "We can go. There's nothing I'd like better than that. I have nothing more to say to Jack today," Isabella stepped confidently. In the car, she explained what had happened to Jack in the supermarket before her mother came in to help. In the family car, she felt safe and protected again. But her heart was still pounding wildly with excitement. When they got back home, her dad had just returned from the precinct. He, too, noticed immediately that something was wrong with Isabella. Annabelle informed him of the incident at the supermarket, while together they carried the grocery bags from the car into the house. Isabella preferred to retire to her room to call Benjamin in Mississippi. The phone call did her good, so her body continued to calm down. For more than a full hour, the two talked and laughed on the cell phone. The usually bubbly Isabella later listened to meditation music and did yoga to it. Her parents looked in on her in the room, but didn't want to bring up the subject. All they cared about was seeing if their daughter was okay or needed to be taken back to the hospital. Katy was currently at work and never came by. Isabella lay back on her bed after her yoga workout while the meditation music continued to play. The slightly sleepy sounds of the meditation made her dizzy and she dozed off.

13.

She began to dream ...

The pianist played on the old piano in the Western Saloon. The pretty dancers stood on the stage and threw their long legs up in the air. The male crowd was going wild. Drunken patrons sat on old wooden chairs with their whiskeys and smoked, played cards, cheered on the girls, or beat each other half to death. This was the western town of Golden Hills, which except for cowboys and rowdies made the search for the precious gold worth living. Men who ran their saloons and cooked beans alongside beautiful stage dancers. Hot-blooded show performer Isabella da Goldie carried a double burden at once. Two suitors were vying for the beauty's favor. The noble and wild cowboy Benjamin against the shrewd and cunning merchant Jack. Who should she choose? And more importantly, for whom did her heart beat? In the evening all hell broke loose again in the saloon. One drunker than the other. "Bella, tonight you throw your skirt up as high as you can. Your admirers and the other men will freak out," advised her dancer Gloria, whose red lipstick was, as always, applied far too thickly. Isabella da Goldie was more of the quiet type in private. Apart from dancing, she had only one intention, namely to find the man of her dreams in order to start a family with him in the future. On stage, the dancers gave their all, being cheered and touched by the smelly, drunk guests. "They're my favorite when they're just playing cards," laughed the oldest of the dancers, Maria Garcia. Merchant Jack, who had just made another advantageous deal with a drunken rowdy, now turned his attention to his greatest enemy and adversary; sidekick and cowboy Benjamin. All the while, he sat silently in front of the stage, watching Isabella dance. He pulled off his cowboy hat to pay tribute to Isabella da Goldie. Jack grabbed Benjamin's shoulder from behind and whispered in his ear, "You'll never get her. Isabella is mine. What's she going to do with a poor slob like you?" Benjamin looked Kaufmann Jack deeply and seriously in the eyes. He stood up and motioned manfully. "Leave her alone. You don't deserve her," the cowboy countered. The merchant would not stand for this and challenged Benjamin to a duel. He agreed and casually put his cowboy hat on his head, took another drag on his cigarette before going outside. All the men present lined up around the two enemies. Merchant Jack on one side and Cowboy Benjamin on the other. The dancers whistled and marveled at the announced duel between the two different men. Only Isabella was not in the mood to cheer. She was trembling and her heart was pounding. But for whom? Who was the right one? Who couldn't she live without? The tension rose and the warm air made the red floor swirl with every step. Isabella's heart almost slipped into her skirt with worry, she couldn't watch the immature game and put her hands in front of her eyes. The two men were already holding the revolvers in their hands, ready to pull the colt any second. Isabella thought to herself that she would most likely lose both men in the nonsensical shootout. An inner voice spoke to her, "Benjamin stay with me!" The spectators continued cheering and cheering for the opponents ...

"Isabella wake up," Thomas shook his daughter. Annabelle lay a damp cloth on her warm forehead. Slowly, the twenty-year-old awoke from her dream. Her mother turned off the meditation music. "You don't believe what I dreamed? Such bullshit ..." Isa didn't realize that the dream meant more than bullshit. In the dream, she chose Benjamin. It was perhaps this that she also wanted with all her heart in real life.

14.

After Isabella slowly digested the dream and also came to terms with the fight in the supermarket, Jack was no longer the potential dream man for her. She recovered from the strain around him and began to move on with her life. She enjoyed time at home with her parents and Katy. She continued to go walking and do yoga as usual. With Benji she talked on the phone every day, with Ava she continued to keep pen-pals. The young woman continued to read her romance novel every free minute. She became completely absorbed in the story of the two lovers. She was carried away and felt the story literally inside her. It was as if she were in the middle of it herself. As she read the novel, her creativity grew to look at people from a different perspective and to question things. She had to think again about the unfulfilled theme of her missing grandmother. While reading the novel and thinking about her grandmother, who was perhaps no longer alive, she blanked out everything around her. Her outside world was nonexistent to her in those moments. "Isa, it's not good if you only fixate on the book and don't notice the rest of your surroundings. I know Ava is a great woman and if you like, I would like to read the novel when you finish it," Annabelle suggested. And her mother was right, Isa realized. It didn't matter if one was too absorbed in a book, a movie or a computer game; at some point one should face reality and make one's own life. So she put the novel aside for now and devoted herself to the telephone conversations with Benjamin from Mississippi. She also kept in frequent phone contact with her former roommate from the hospital. Chatting with Katy, family game nights and Chinese food were all part of her daily routine. But deep in her subconscious, the question of her grandmother still lurked. To distract herself, Isabella picked up Ava's novel again to continue reading it. In most books there was often a happy ending, which was usually foreshadowed early on. The novel by her newfound friend Ava also indicated that the story of the two lovers would end well. Inspired by the love story she was reading, the need for an ideal family world and perfection came up in her again. Yes, perfection was a big issue. Isa wanted to feel whole. Not knowing who her grandma was, she didn't feel complete. There was a piece missing that she was able to search for. The missing piece of the puzzle was finally to be filled in and the mystery of the unknown grandmother was to be solved. Only in this way could she find inner peace and her heart would come to rest. Sometimes it felt as if part of the old heart was still beating inside her. Her own heart was removed, but that didn't mean Isabella didn't feel it anymore. She was fine with Mary's heart, it fit. Still, she wondered if she could ever muster the strength to find her own grandmother with that heart? Yes, she would. Isabella decided this inwardly for herself. But for that, she needed her mother, Annabelle. Without her, the heart patient would not be able to find her beloved and sorely missed grandmother. Every time Isabella approached her mother about finding her grandmother, it ended in chaos, arguments, and a hospital stay for the twenty-year-old. Isabella had no desire to end up in the hospital again after that. The fight with boyfriend Jack didn't do her health any good, luckily she stayed away from the hospital after that, but it didn't always have to go that way. She didn't want to risk anything and wanted to take a level-headed approach. This time she wrote a letter to her parents asking for help in finding her grandmother. In the process, she got her feelings off her chest. It was like a kind of writing therapy. Reasoning that before the heart transplant, she had a strong and intimate feeling that her heart was missing someone; the thought remained embedded in her mind and body to this day. She had a new heart, but the desire had remained. Isabella thought perhaps one day she would become a mother herself and then she would like to tell her child about her great-grandmother. Her heart could only miss the unknown grandma, because otherwise all the people in her life were present. The Jack and Benjamin thing would work itself out, too. She was sure of that. She thoughtfully finished writing the letter. Hoping that her parents would support her in her search, especially after the surgery had gone well and she seemed reasonably okay. She placed the letter on her mother's sleeping pillow that evening. Tomorrow she would have certainty if her parents would be willing to join her in looking for her grandmother?

"Honey, we'll talk about your letter tonight when your dad gets home from work," was all Annabelle would say on the subject. Isabella had spent the day coming up with a plan for the search. This time she would find her grandma and nothing could stop her. Katy painted a sign in solidarity with her best friend.

On it was written: *Search for my grandmother!* The sign was still at Katy's home, but she showed it to Isa via Internet video. Motivated by her best friend's help, Isabella was certain that her parents would now also help. At least, she took it as a guess. When her dad came home from the police station that evening, he discussed the matter with his wife for a long time. The two discussed the letter while Isa waited in her room. She was on pins and needles, eager to hear her parents' response. 'Please no fighting now. Just help me,' the organized young woman thought to herself. Before she was about to go down to her parents, she made a phone call to Katy, who voiced her opinion, 'Let me know what your parents said and if they will help you? I'll be honest, they didn't want to know about the issue until now and had even closed their minds about it. Why would they change their minds now of all times?" A little irritated, Isabella crept downstairs to the living room to eavesdrop on her parents' conversation. They noticed their daughter and immediately stopped discussing. "There you are," her mother acted quite surprised when Isa stood in the doorway. 'What is it now? Answer me at last,' the young woman spoke in her mind. Annabelle and Thomas stood wordlessly in their own living room for seconds. Isabella could wait no longer, it burst out of her. She could no longer control herself and began to speak loudly: 'Have you made up your minds? How long am I supposed to wait?" The parents never perceived their daughter so loud before, unless she laughed loudly and heartily. That's why they wanted to calm Isabella down first. Annabelle spoke in a self-controlled tone, "We are grateful to you for your openness and the letter. And we can understand you, too. But that's not the point." Isabella only got angrier, "Then what is it about? Please tell us!" Again the parents were silent for a few seconds. Annabelle took another breath before arguing, as she always did before: "It's my mother and not yours. I'm your mother, you have a father and that's the most important thing. I have to deal with it, that's why I'm done with the subject. And I've explained it to you so many times. I have researched and received no information. That's the end of the subject for me. As I said, your grandpa was a black man and he is sadly deceased. Your grandma is a white woman and certainly very old. I am assuming that she is no longer alive. I don't know anything more about her or the situation. My adoptive parents did everything for me and I couldn't have been better off. I went to college, got married, and had you. And I'm asking you now for the last time, Isabella .... This is my subject and not yours. Take leave of it, and henceforth concentrate on your own life and around your health." She felt completely misunderstood and left alone with the subject. She experienced certainty. Her parents would not and could not help her in her search. Her mother had long since finished with the subject and Isabella should do the same. Annabelle made her understand that this was no longer an issue for her and that she would never change her mind. For her the subject was through, but for Isabella the subject was just beginning.

The rain outside fell down on the streets and the houses. The drops pelted from the sky, the air grew colder, nature cleansed itself. At home with Isabella, the twenty-year-old raged inwardly with anger and helplessness. What should she do now? Let it escalate again, brought the last time already nothing but trouble. Her mother had made up her mind and that was clear. So Isabella had only one thing left to do. Search on her own. Katy didn't want to drag her into this. Her best friend should concentrate on her work and studies and of course continue to come over for a chat. That had always been enough for her so far. She couldn't rely on Jack anymore, and Benjamin was just getting to know her. To him, she was the heart patient who was getting his aunt's heart transplanted. Isabella considered this fact enough information for a person she wanted to get to know. Had she confronted him directly with the family's fate, it would likely have been overwhelming for the young, friendly man from Mississippi. Although Isabella firmly believed that Benji would have stood by her if he had known the concern. Left to her own devices,

Isabella thus went to her room and packed her backpack. Determined that she had to deal with the situation on her own. The rain outside was getting heavier and did not stop. While Isabella was putting the essentials for the search into her backpack, she heard her parents arguing downstairs in the living room. Annabelle had blocked any help in the search for the grandmother in the conversation with her daughter, but her father apparently stood by his daughter. She could hear that from the argument. Thomas seriously considered whether help could be made available to his daughter? "Maybe my guys from the Bureau can get some information for our daughter? That would at least be a consideration. Don't you think?" Annabelle looked displeased, "That's ridiculous. The police have more important things to do than find my mother, who probably isn't even alive anymore. This is completely absurd." The argument between the parents continued. This did not stop Isabella from continuing to pack her backpack for the search. True, the quarrel between her beloved parents weighed heavily on her mind; after all, she had wished it otherwise. But it was just the way it was. Isa resolutely went downstairs to the living room and told her parents that she was leaving the house now to look for her grandmother. "On her own," she called it. Startled by their daughter's plan, the parents ended the argument. "Where are you going? It's raining outside. She could be anywhere or already dead. The situation is hopeless," Annabelle was very worried about her daughter. Since she herself never got to meet her biological mother, she didn't want to lose her greatest treasure, her only daughter. Without another word, the determined young rebel ran out the door and into the downpour. The destination was uncertain; her grandmother's whereabouts could theoretically be anywhere in the whole wide world. Even the size of the United States of America seemed overwhelmingly large for this uncertain quest. So where to start? The questions not quite pronounced in her mind, Isabella was soaked from top to bottom. Her parents were enormously worried because of the heart transplant, combined with high risks, so they also ran out to look for their daughter. But it was too late, Isabella was long out of sight. Without any clue, the young woman continued to walk through the rainy streets. This was not without danger, for her heart donor Mary had herself died on a street. Isa kept this terrible accident in the back of her mind as she set off in search of her grandmother. Unthinkingly, she walked across the endless streets. After an hour of senseless traversing in the rain, Isabella stopped. She sensed that her grandmother was still alive. That's why she shouted outside in the dark through the rain, as loud as she could: "I feel that you are still alive! Now tell me, where are you?"

After the seeker's strength slowly waned, she sheltered at a store. 'My heart, just don't abandon me now,' she talked to herself in her mind as she stood trembling under the canopy of a store with blue lips tarnished. 'Come, we'll take the car. It won't do any good. Out here we'll catch our deaths," Thomas and Annabelle ran back to the house to put on dry clothes. Then they set off in the car in search of their daughter. Annabelle was as if she was remote-controlled. She did not want to lose her daughter at any price, she blamed herself for not offering Isabella to support her in the search, even if the search seemed hopeless for herself. The two drove around for a full hour, but their only daughter was nowhere to be found. "What are we going to do? I'm sure she's not at Jack's. We should ring Katy's doorbell, even though it's late. It's still worth a try," Annabelle spoke urgently. Thomas drove straight to the house where Katy lived with her parents. Her father opened the front door and spoke to Isabella's parents. Katy joined them when she heard their voices. Friendly and courteous, the couple was invited inside. They shared their concerns and fears with Katy's family. Unfortunately, Isabella was not to be found there. Their daughter's best friend made the suggestion to call Isabella on her cell phone. Several times she rang her friend. Isa didn't answer her cell phone, which worried her parents even more. "I hope nothing happened to her. I would never forgive myself," Annabelle burst into tears. Katy's mother handed Isabella's mother tissues and made tea for everyone. "We can't file a missing person report at police headquarters for another 24 hours. I hope we will have found her by then," Thomas took his wife in his arms. Isabella wanted to keep searching even during

167

the night. Dripping wet, she headed for the subway, here at least she was sitting in the dry. Isa hoped to receive an inspiration from above. But this night she should have no luck. Across the city, the journey continued unsuccessfully on the moving subway. At the same time, Thomas contacted a colleague at work who also knew Isabella well. He asked him to keep an eye out for his daughter when he was on patrol.

15.

The next day was still rainy. Isabella was coughing constantly, her heart was not well at all. She got hungry and thirsty during the long search through the big city. She was tired and exhausted at the same time. Had she not been able to sleep the night in the subway. The fear of being robbed was just too great. And waiting for a sign from above seemed too important to the searcher. So Isa continued to walk around outside. Her clothes were already soaked again and still. If lung disease was added to the mix, the young woman probably wouldn't survive. Fear rose and hope disappeared. It would be better the other way around. The situation seemed more hopeless than ever. The heart patient felt like she had to give up and bury her dream of finding her own grandmother inside. She had come through the heart transplant well and was about to risk everything by going out on her own for far too long in the rain and stress. Her stockings, even her underpants and bra felt like she had just come out of the swimming pool. The coughing got louder and stronger. On her way to a public restroom, she saw some homeless people sitting on the side of the road. Isabella knew she had a home, but she also just felt like someone without a residence. She wandered around the area and found nothing. Wet, sick, with hunger in her stomach and much thirst. She felt incredibly sorry for the people on the street, because behind every homeless person there was always a story. She had hardly any money with her, but she wanted to give something away. She approached a homeless man who seemed particularly desolate. A few dollars she placed in his empty coffee cup. "God bless you–God bless you," the homeless man wished Isabella. Throwing him a smile, she then sought out the public restroom. Here she found a brief moment of peace and privacy. She warmed herself under a fan dryer. Finally, it was her head's turn. Drying her hair took a lot of time, but the effort was worth it. Then drank from the tap and went outside again. Halfway dry and fresh, Isabella went to a stand where she bought a snack to eat. Out of hunger, she immediately devoured the meal. Although it was hard to walk around the streets looking for a needle in a haystack, Isabella still had no intention of returning home. She wanted to look a little further. And so she continued on her way into the unknown. In doing so, she suppressed the fact that she had become extremely wet beforehand and had even developed an elevated temperature in the meantime. She continued on her way and was surprised by the ringing of her cell phone. She saw her mother's number on the display. She briefly wondered whether she should answer it at all? Isabella had always been a good daughter and never wanted to start a fight on purpose. She knew how worried her parents were about her. So she answered it. Isa felt her mother Annabelle's tears and despair through the phone. Feeling guilty, she talked to her mum so kindly as if there had never been a fight. Annabelle was overjoyed to hear the voice of her only daughter, who was also sick. And she now knew that Isabella was staying in town and not moving states. Her dad also spoke to her. Being a police officer, he knew the dangers that were constantly out there in the big city, so of course he didn't want her to continue to be out there alone as a young woman. Especially not at night. Isabella sincerely assured them that she would be home soon. As she continued to communicate with her parents on her cell phone, she couldn't believe her eyes. She saw her boyfriend Jack driving up the street in his car. He too had noticed Isabella and stopped the car on the side of the road without getting out. Isabella got a shock when she saw Jack unexpectedly. It was raining again and the sky was dark and eerie. He rolled down his car window and called provocatively to Isabella, "Are you on the phone with your new lover again?" She couldn't and wouldn't believe what she just heard. "Mom, I have to go. I'll get back to you later." And pressed the sign on the red handset to hang up. "What do you mean lover? I've always been faithful to you. So stop yelling such lies around town," Isabella countered while standing drenched in the rain again. Jack just left his girlfriend standing there in the wet. He didn't offer her a ride home in a warm car. Instead, more accusations followed on his part. Had love turned to hate? It seemed so. Jack was still sitting in his dry car, yelling out through the open window. With all the accusations, Isabella felt worse and worse and noticed how she was almost falling over. Briefly, she closed her eyes and clung to a street pillar. 'I'm not going to do this anymore. I'm going to tell him now, if it's the last thing I do today,' Isabella walked boldly towards Jack's car. 'You know what Jack? I've had enough. I've had to listen to enough of you. You don't stand by me and the life I lead anymore. You don't give a damn about my desires. And that's why I don't care now what might become of us. You go your way and I'll go mine. It's better this way. I'm breaking up with you. Good luck, Jack." That had hit home. Without making a face, Jack accepted the verdict. Nevertheless, he voiced his opinion. He got out of his car and complained about the rain, which he suddenly noticed standing outside without a roof over his head. 'Spoiled brat,' the twenty-year-old thought to herself. 'You're breaking up with me? What a joke. I've only been with you out of pity. Because of nothing else. Just out of pity. You haven't been my type for a long time anyway," the young man, who had been with Isabella since their school days, boasted. He wanted to hurt her, he had no other intention. Due to his demanding studies and his perfectionism, her former boyfriend had changed. He had been a normal and nice boy in his school days. Growing older turned him into a showy student. Deep in her heart, Isabella wished for him to be happy. The young woman let the teasing stand without comment. Since Jack was no longer offered a target, he got into his car and drove away. She briefly looked after him and came to the conclusion that her decision had been well made. The two spent many years together and also went through hard times due to Isabella's chronic heart muscle inflammation. Jack had definitely changed for the worse. It was raining hard and the sky was colored as if black. You couldn't tell the tears on Isabella's face from the rain. She had to return home or she would collapse here on the street. Her heart and lungs would not stand the wetness on the road much longer. Isabella wanted to live. In order not to lose herself in the end, she looked for the quickest way back home. Without calling her parents, she set off alone through the dark, wet streets. The walk took two hours. When Isabella arrived home, she was so exhausted that she thought her life would soon be over. Annabelle and Thomas were already coming to meet her. At that moment she knew how nice it was to have parents. Parents who cared and worried about you. They freed their daughter from her dripping wet clothes, made her a warm bath and a tea to go with it. Then they laid Isa on the couch and realized with horror how badly she was feeling. Isabella was panting heavily from coughing and had a high fever. "I'll call the ambulance," there was no discussion between the parents. It was clear to both of them that their daughter was in mortal danger. A few minutes later, the ambulance was already at their door and loaded the twenty-year-old in the back. Annabelle was allowed to ride in the ambulance with her sick daughter, and Thomas followed behind in the family car. When they arrived at the hospital, Isabella was immediately taken to the heart center. A kind of special clinic where she had almost lived as a patient before. The competent nurse put Isabella on an IV.

All the examinations started all over again. A drug to lower the fever and other necessary medicines were introduced into her body. For a short time, Isabella even had to be on the ventilator. "I don't want to lose her. Oh, Lordy. She has to stay with us," Annabelle fell into Thomas' arms, crying. "The Lord won't take her yet. He can't let that happen. Our sunshine stays here," he comforted his wife. But even he was not convinced this time.

Their daughter was placed in the intensive care unit of the heart clinic that same day. The fight for her life had long since begun. Never before had the parents feared so much for Isabella's life. The search for a suitable heart donor was also enormously stressful, but there was hope. This time, the parents were not so sure. The unfulfilled search for her grandmother became Isabella's life's mission, from which her parents could not dissuade her. That's why the fear was there every day. Only from the hospital, there at least she could not escape. For the first time, the parents were happy to know their daughter was in the hospital. After a few days in the intensive care unit, the young woman had survived the worst and was allowed to move to the normal hospital ward. "She has been given a third life. I hope she is aware of that?", Thomas spoke to his wife. The first life was before the heart transplant, the second began when she got Mary's heart, the third life started when she was allowed to leave the intensive care unit. And infinite lives were not available to her either. But apparently enough guardian angels to shepherd her again each time. Of course, the well-known and leading senior physician wanted to know how it could come to pass that Isabella was suddenly in such bad shape? The parents told the doctor about the family fate that had been haunting them for ages. "The search for her grandmother will put her in the grave yet. I want to avoid that at all costs," Annabelle told the doctor. "I'm very sorry for what they've been through as a family. Isabella seems to care a lot about knowing who her grandmother is and if she's still alive? Many patients look for a new task after a long stay in hospital, a task that is often much too lofty. Humanly, I can understand her daughter. But as a physician, I have to warn her urgently not to continue as before. But you know that," the senior physician warned. Annabelle and Thomas looked at a loss. "Doctor, what should we do now? She's so fixated on meeting her unknown grandmother that she just takes off. She leaves no matter if it's raining or storming. No matter how dangerous it is outside. We can't stop her. She would also run away at night. And then we can't get to her anymore. We constantly try to talk to her, but in vain. Her body has already been through a lot, and I'm afraid that since she was very sick, her heart won't take it much longer." The usually strong father and policeman had reached the end of his strength and knew no more advice. "It's very hard on this to give the perfect answer or the one tip. There probably isn't one either. As soon as her daughter is discharged from the hospital, she has to return to the clinic here once a week for a checkup. And I also recommend psychotherapy for her once a week. She can do that here at the clinic. She comes to therapy and then goes back home. It's best to accompany your daughter to the appointments and wait until she's done. I am sorry. That's all I can advise at the moment. She needs to take it easy and get some rest. In talk therapy, she can give her feelings a framework," the doctor replied very understanding and sympathetic to the family's situation. A little relieved by the suggestions about their daughter's near future, the couple regained hope. Katy and her parents also came to visit the runaway in the normal infirmary. When the two girls were alone for a short moment, Isabella told her best friend about the meeting with Jack on the street and about Isabella breaking up with him. "Well, finally, it's about time. I couldn't stand him anymore. And he was so nice then. You did a good job of that. He didn't deserve you, the way he's changed for the worse." Katy stood by her friend and understood her decision to break up with Jack. Isa also told her parents about the messy meeting with Jack and that they were now no longer a couple. Annabelle and Thomas always liked Jack, but lately they didn't have a good feeling about him anymore. The separation was also a relief for Isabella's parents and brought peace to the family.

A week later, Isabella was allowed to leave the clinic. The doctors had already told her what to do next. The thought of looking for her grandmother on her own was no longer relevant for the pretty woman with a heart condition. She had understood that this was her last chance. And that's why she did what the doctors asked her to do. She went to the clinic every week to have her heart and general health checked. She also took her mother to the hospital once a week to see Dr. Blum for psychotherapy. Mr. Blum was a good therapist who patiently addressed Isabella's concerns. The major building blocks of her life were looked at. Many topics were addressed, such as Isabella's school days, her ex-boyfriend Jack, her chronic heart muscle inflammation, her transplant, her relationship with her parents, her best friends Katy, Ava and Benjamin, and of course, her desire to meet her grandmother. The therapy did her good and continued, as did the examinations in the heart clinic. Calm slowly returned at home. Everyday life took hold of the family. Isabella knew what she had done with her runaway action and what fears she had caused in her parents. Between dinner and watching TV, Isabella sincerely apologized to her parents for the past few months. The three of them embraced each other. Nothing and no one could separate them. Isa felt healthier and accepted in her family again. Thomas and Annabelle were content with life and thanked God every day that their daughter survived another hospital visit. Still, the circumstances of the last few weeks were taking their toll on her. Her body needed a lot of rest, which she gave in to, and she slept a surprising amount during the first time, even during the day. She refueled her body with energy while she slept. The difficult heart transplant, the many arguments with Jack, then the separation, the search for her grandmother and the elopement had all been major stress factors for the twenty-year-old. Her body regenerated while she slept, her heart began to settle into her body anew, beating and finding its way. Normalcy and routine made everyday life easier for everyone. Benjamin tried to call Isabella daily from Mississippi. At one point, she answered and told Benji that she had suffered a physical relapse and therefore needed to rest a lot. But the truth was different. The termination of the relationship was not long ago. She thought it would be smart to process the breakup first and work it out with herself. Only after that she wanted to get back in touch with Benjamin. Benji wished her a speedy recovery, he did not want to disturb her recovery. She carried the heart of his deceased aunt, therefore Mary was a part of and in her. Isabella was going to get well with Mary's heart. If he lost Isa, then his aunt would also be dead for good. He didn't want that to happen. He left his Louisiana acquaintance alone, hoping to hear from her again soon. The weeks passed for Isabella with rest, yoga, Katy's visits, the weekly presentation at the clinic, and therapy with Doctor Blum. Even to Ava, she wrote the same thing she told Benjamin. She had relapsed, was in the hospital, and now needed to recover. Ava was as kind as Benjamin and wished her all the best as well as physical recovery. Ava wrote about news from Mississippi and asked if Isa had finished reading the novel yet? There was something, Isabella remembered. She continued to read the romance novel with anticipation. In the evenings, she often played Scrabble with her parents, laughing a lot. The vocabulary game kept Isa fit and was a nice activity for their family life together in Louisiana. She was about to put a tricky word on the board when Thomas spoke up, "Isabella, your mother and I have thought of something for you. It's in consultation with Doctor Blum." Isa sat tensely in the chair, waiting to hear what her parents said. "We know you've only had one issue in the past besides the heart transplant. Since you got a donor heart, there is only one issue left. Namely, finding your grandmother. You know that your mother has long since finished with the subject. Actually, we wanted to leave it at that. Our wish was simply for you to get well. Nevertheless, we would like to make you a little concession." Isabella jumped up from her chair and shouted loudly, "Yes!" Annabelle tried to calm her down as Thomas continued to speak, "But don't expect too much. We've decided that we're going to take another trip with you to the Louisiana adoption office to find out. We've been there before, maybe we'll have better luck this time. Well Isabella is that something?" The twenty-year-old fell around her parents' necks, beaming with joy. And Annabelle added, "We made an appointment there for tomorrow morning." Isa jumped on the couch and bounced around there with glee. "Hey don't get too wild. Think about your heart. You want to be fit tomorrow. Don't you?" grinned Thomas. Isabella stood on the couch like a winner who was about to receive a trophy. The evening could not have ended more beautifully. The family looked forward to the next day with anticipation.

A breakfast of freshly squeezed OJ, bacon, toast, cereal and egg was to fortify the family before they headed into the jungle of the office. All three donned formal outfits. "We look like we work at the bank or at the insurance company," Isabella marveled in front of the mirror. Her mother looked at her seriously, "And don't be sad if we don't get any information." Isa took her mother in her arms and said, "I'm already so grateful that you two are going through this together with me today. No matter what the outcome." Isabella had matured and grown up. Promptly at 10 a.m., the three of them stood outside the entrance to the Louisiana Office of Adoption. A long car ride had already been completed by the family. Thomas had traded shifts with a colleague especially for this purpose. Before they went inside, they took their daughter by the hand. Up the stairs, the door opened and they were already standing in the large building. Annabelle was holding the number she needed for the appointment. Six digits could possibly be the gateway to great happiness. Nervously, they sat down in the waiting area. A digital board displayed the numbers in which row they were allowed to see the officials. The board hung high up, so everyone had to stick their heads over to see the numbers. After a bit of waiting, the time finally came. 686 741 was displayed on the digital board. "That's us," Annabelle spoke, while Isabella was already waiting in the wings. In the conference room, a somewhat portly, black Southern lady greeted her. "What can I do for you today?" A nice, charming invitation for the conversation to come. "Well then, this is so ...," Annabelle began to tell. It was she, after all, who was actually the subject of the conversation. At that time, she was given away by her light-skinned mother and adopted into a new family. The officer listened to the whole story calmly. She did not interject or ask questions. Everything seemed open and Isabella could hardly wait for the answer that was about to come out of the officer's mouth. It seemed infinitely long to her until the lady opened her mouth: "I can see from the files that you have been here before with your husband." Annabelle and Thomas looked at each other in amazement. "Yes. That is correct. However, it was also many years ago," Isabella's mother answered succinctly. The officer in charge was silent for a moment and looked at the three. She looked into their eyes and felt the hope that was in them. "I'm sorry. I cannot give you any other information today, as the person before me did. Means, I have no more information about it. The adoption was too long ago. You are 60 years old. They were adopted shortly after birth. They were not even one year old. So the event was 59 years ago.

I'm sorry. We don't keep the files that long," the employee from the office, felt sorry for this incident. Isabella didn't want to give up and asked, "But isn't there some other place where the file still exists? Or another office where we can get information?" The officer shook her head and had to answer in the negative: "Unfortunately not. If I knew anything or had a clue, I would tell them. In those days, you wrote everything by hand. Or with a typewriter. So I can't find anything about their case in our database. I am truly sorry." Isabella was up to her neck in pity and regret. The family thanked the lady kindly and left the meeting room.

16.

This time Isabella was not the sad one at all, but her mother Annabelle. For years she suppressed the pain and her hope. Only through Isabella's wish did everything come up again in her. She did it only for her daughter and only realized too late that she had done it for herself. And was deeply disappointed again. For a brief moment she let hope take hold of her. Thomas, who had known his wife for many years, knew the pain she was now enduring. Isabella and he embraced mother and wife in the parking lot. The ride home remained silent, no one could or dared say anything. Annabelle had a lump in her throat. Now that they got the ball rolling, Thomas wasn't about to give up and move on. "We'll find another way," he was sure. "Didn't you hear what the woman said? There's nothing more we can do. The case is too long ago. It's too late and we have to accept that," Annabelle tried to keep her composure. But she was broken inside. Isabella, on the other hand, could say nothing at all. She had always been the leader of the grandmother search. Slowly she understood what deep pain was in her mother. A pain that she had endured for almost 60 years and threatened to break. Isabella was deeply ashamed to have started this subject. She didn't want to look any further, but her parents were now emotionally involved in the issue again. Once home, Thomas and Annabelle discussed how to proceed, but they were interrupted by their daughter: "Oh, you know, maybe I don't care so much about the subject after all. I have no problem if we stop now and go on with our lives." The parents could not believe their eyes and ears. That wasn't their daughter standing there right now saying that? The situation seemed completely surreal. Isabella was going to stop looking for her own grandmother? The parents couldn't believe that after their daughter had searched for the unknown grandma on her own like a fighter, risking her life.

The next evening, Thomas came home from the police station with an idea: "I have a plan. There's a lawyer. He's a three-hour drive from here, but he's supposed to be the best in his field. He's a specialist lawyer and in the field of adoption. My colleague told me that he is known far beyond the country's borders and has even made an appearance on television. I will call him tomorrow immediately and ask for an appointment and for the costs. If he's that good, I'm sure he won't be cheap. But we'll work it out." Isabella stood there rooted to the spot and wordless. There she had started a topic. A topic she no longer wanted to pursue, because of her mother's emotional state. Annabelle was also wordless, but still hugged her husband as a sign of gratitude. "We'll figure this out together. I promise you," he added. The doorbell rang, Katy arrived as if on cue. Isabella immediately led her to her room. "What's the matter? Am I not even allowed to say hello to your parents anymore, or why are you in such a hurry?" Katy felt caught off guard. "No. Listen like this. Back then and until recently, I really wanted to meet my grandmother and introduce her to our family. That was my fondest wish. I would have done anything for it. And I did. I almost died in the process. And now it's the other way around. I have realized that there is no more chance and that my mother has already gone through hell for it. I don't want to hurt her any more. The funny thing is: now my parents want to keep looking. Although the adoption officer has already told us that the case was too long ago and they have no more information about it. And still my dad really wants to keep looking. My mom doesn't say much anymore. She's probably all broken up," Isa explained in detail about the latest events. The two discussed the family's situation until it got late and dark. Katy went home because she had to work the next morning.

The next day, Annabelle was barely responsive. Isabella had never seen her mother, a social worker who advocated and stood up for others, like this. She didn't know what to say to her mother and stayed in her room most of the time. Until her father came home from work that evening. He didn't have any good news in his luggage. "Darling. Here's the thing ...", you could tell by the look in Annabelle's eyes that she was expecting some unpleasant news. Thomas continued speaking, "I first spoke to the lawyer's secretary on the phone. The lawyer himself called me back five hours later. It's like jinxed. Apparently, a lot of people have problems with a former adoption. At least he's so busy that he can't take on new clients for another 10 to 12 months. He didn't want to give me any hope. Then he asked if we can wait that long and he should put us on the waiting list? Then he will get back to us in a year. I told him I would discuss it at home first and then get back to him. He sounded nice and competent, but he's also busy. Typical specialist lawyer." Hard as a rock, his wife Annabelle replied, "No. That's enough. I don't want any more!" She disappeared upstairs to the bedroom.

17.

Plagued by reproaches and a guilty conscience, Isabella would have preferred to continue hiding in her room. She looked in the mirror and didn't want to be like that. She didn't want to be the daughter who made her mother fall into despair. Instead of going back to her room, she preferred to visit Annabelle in her bedroom. Her mother was lying sideways on the bed with her eyes closed. Isabella quietly and slowly crept up to the bed and lay with her sleeping mother. Annabelle noticed this and tentatively put her arm around Isabella as if to protect her daughter. As warm as a blanket, Isa felt wrapped under her mother's arm. The two women fell asleep sheltered in the master bedroom. Thomas came up later and put a soft sleeping blanket over his two treasures. He had not seen his daughter and wife lying together so intimately for a very long time. The bond between mother and daughter was about to be brought back to life. 'At last. At least this is working. 'Thank God,' Thomas thanked his wife for the regained love between his two wives. Isabella had survived the difficult heart transplant and several setbacks. But the dogged search for the unknown grandmother turned Isabella into an opponent of her own mother, because she did not want to search with her. After a long time, the parents agreed to a first step in the joint search, but it also came to nothing. To experience

Annabelle's pain again was even worse for Isabella than the fact of not having found her grandmother.

Like a lightning strike, an idea hit the twenty-year-old. She wanted to continue searching secretly for her mother. 'If I go in search of my biological grandmother unnoticed and I don't have any results to show, then it won't hurt her as much again,' was the young fighter's plan. No sooner said than done. Two days later, when her father was on patrol, Isabella announced to her mother that she was going for a walk outside. A little white lie, so to speak. She took her walking sticks with her as a cover and a backpack in which she put something to write. "See you later, Mum," she called to Annabelle and disappeared. Without any detours, Isa went straight to an Internet café. She quickly found a quiet place and promptly sat down. Since you can find anything on the Internet, she thought to herself, highly motivated, the World Wide Web would certainly help her too. The worldwide web was to be tapped. Isabella concentrated on researching her missing grandmother. The heart patient felt like a freelance journalist while searching the web. She did not find what she was looking for, but did not want to give up so quickly. There were many articles about adoptions on the Internet. Also about fates that were also some decades ago. Racism was also a topic of discussion. She also discovered similar cases of couples of different origins on the Internet. Meticulously and carefully she read each article to possibly learn a little information about her own grandparents and their history. But unfortunately, this was not the case. For hours, Isabella was engrossed in the comparable provisions of other people. When her neck began to ache, she took a short break. She gently stroked the back of her neck with her hand; her eyes were tired from constantly staring at the screen. To distract herself, she briefly looked out the window. "I don't believe it now," Isabella rose from her chair and looked out a little closer. She had not been mistaken. Out on the street, she saw her ex-boyfriend Jack flirting with the Hillary Spencer she knew. "He sure changed his tune fast," Isa realized. The situation was strange for the young woman to see; after all, she had been with Jack for years. Still, it was okay with her and even felt good. She inwardly wished him all the best and was sure she had made the right decision. She didn't feel any jealousy or envy towards the two of them. As long as she could see them out of the window, she looked. Curiosity made itself felt in her. When all she saw were cars on the streets, she sat back in the chair and continued to research her grandmother. She typed places and names into the keyboard, keywords, parts of her story, anything she could think of. She searched for a possible answer in the keys. Unfortunately, this search was also unsuccessful. Only one important piece of information was to come to her. Increased articles were written about private detectives. Some people, when searching for missing relatives, hired a detective to find the person they were looking for.

Often with success. Isabella took this tip to heart. She searched the Internet for a suitable private detective in the area and also for agencies that specialized in such cases. 'Oh no. The agencies are way too expensive. I'll stick with the detective. I'm sure he has good training in that field,' she thought to herself. Then she packed her things, took her walking sticks and paid. At home, her mother was already waiting for her with a hot chocolate. Fingers crossed, she gushed about how great it was to go walking outside. "Honey, I'm glad you're feeling better by now. Keep it up! Oh yes. Katy called, she wants you to call her back when you get home," her mother told her. "I will mum," Isabella gave her mother a kiss on the cheek and went upstairs to her room. From her cell phone she talked to her best friend. Isa told her all about the internet search and about seeing Jack with the pretty and popular Hillary Spencer. "What a jerk that he traded you for that cocky Spencer. It's his own fault," Katy, as usual, didn't mince words. The young women gossiped and gossiped a bit about ex Jack and his new flame.

Thomas came home from work with a big bouquet of flowers. Annabelle stood in the kitchen looking longingly familiar and loving into her husband's eyes. "These are for you. Because every day I'm thankful to have you," and handed his wife the gorgeous bouquet of fragrant flowers. "These are beautiful. I thank you. And I want to apologize," Annabelle began to speak, but Thomas interrupted her, "No. I have to apologize. I just caught you off guard. I only meant well with the specialist lawyer for adoption, but I also know that the search has torn open old wounds in you again. Unfortunately, I thought about that too late. You have experienced such pain in the past because we didn't get anywhere with the search. And at some point we left it and continued to live our wonderful life. And for that life, I want to say thank you." Annabelle began to cry, "And I couldn't imagine a better man by my side than you." The couple kissed intimately and spent the rest of the evening together. A day later, Isabella swindled her mother for the second time. With the excuse that she was going to visit Katy, she left the house. She carefully stowed the note with the private detective's address in her purse. The bus number 057 drove the bright young woman in the direction of the detective agency. An old building with brown tiles and green wooden door was to be her destination. The sign at the entrance read: Private Detective B. Carter, awarded the 2018 gold star of all detective agencies.

Isabella looked impressed and opened the green wooden door expectantly. Inside was a bustle of activity. The lady at the front desk was detached and not particularly polite: "What's up?" That was all she could bring out in her friendliness. "I'm Isabella and I'd like to come in for an interview with Mr. Carter," Isa revealed. "Have a seat in the waiting room. You will be called then," Again there were short, curt instructions from the receptionist. Isabella sat down on the brown leather chair in the indicated room. A carafe of fresh water and mint was ready for customers. So was the daily newspaper. Black and white photos of the detective's work hung on the walls, framed in gold picture frames. Cameras, recording devices, old hats, cigars, whiskey, cars, fine coats on coat racks. The walls were adorned with several black and white motifs from the life of Mr. Carter and his work. His deep voice, including a smoker's cough, could be heard clearly all the way into the waiting room. He seemed very busy. He was constantly heard on the phone or receiving clients in his office. Then finally it was Isabella's turn. She put everything into the highly praised private detective. A white man in a smart suit who could just as easily have passed for a bon vivant. All his important and prominent contacts hung as photos on the walls. Also photographed in black and white. In a smoky voice he asked, "Young lady, how can I help you?" The answer was clear to her and she would have loved to reply, "By finding my grandmother." To rush ahead so quickly seemed a bit cheeky to her. She wanted to take it slower, "I'm looking for my grandmother. My mother Annabelle was put up for adoption shortly after she was born or after a few months? We live here in Louisiana. But it may be that her birth parents lived somewhere else. My mother had me late, she is already 60 years old. So I am not sure if my biological grandmother is still alive? My grandfather was a black, he must be dead by now according to our knowledge. All I know about my grandmother is that she is a white one." Isabella continued to speak and she felt she was in good hands with Mr. Carter and his team. Thoughtfully, the private investigator replied, "Isabella, this could be difficult. But it's not impossible. I've been able to solve some complicated cases all over the United States. That's what I'm here for." Isabella could hardly believe her luck until she heard the next words. He continued, "For my effort and work, I charge $5,000 up front. The rest will be given to them with my final bill to be paid at that time." Her breath caught in her throat at this and she nearly fell out of her chair. Politely, she asked, "The rest?" As if easily and naturally, he replied, "Yes. The $5,000 is just a down payment. The rest of the money, depending on how long I'm on her case, you'll have to wire to me then." Mr. Carter leaned back in his office chair and began to give credit to his smoker's cough. He lit his next cigar. The cloud of smoke drifted directly into Isabella's face. With her hands, she tried to blow the stinky smoke away as she rose from the chair. "I'll have to see if I have that kind of money available and get back to them. Thanks mister." It was clear to Isabella that she would not be able to come up with that amount of money anytime soon. Clearing his throat and somewhat uninterested, Mr. Carter said goodbye to her, "Isabella, you take a look. And then we'll hear from you." With her mood dampened, the young woman made her way home, pondering as she drove what she could sell from her room? 'I'll never get that together,' she thought to herself. The negative attitude toward this large amount was no accident. Back home, her parents were sitting in front of the TV watching a program. "Hey honey, how was it with Katy? Everything good?" her dad asked in a good mood. Isabella, introverted, immediately disappeared upstairs. "Yes. All good," she called softly from down the stairs. "I wonder if there's a storm brewing. Hopefully not a fight with Katy?" Annabelle worried. "I don't think so. Nothing can break those two up," her husband replied. Meanwhile, Isabella turned her entire room upside down, searching in vain for private valuables. She didn't want to take anything from her parents, nor did she want to ask them for so much money. She found a necklace that she got as a birthday present. Also she found a ring and a brooch, which she received from her parents for a very good graduation. An old CD collection, equally expensive but used sneakers and her modern TV set. Together, they amounted to less than half the asking price. Isa got into a bad mood. She decided to save the necessary money or maybe take a small job that she could physically do well. That way she would slowly get the money together. Just as she was about to check her cell phone for side jobs, her father knocked on the door: "Tomorrow is the weekend. We have a great surprise for you. We hope you don't have anything important planned yet." Isa was pleased, but would rather look for a suitable job. "Uh. Well. So ... Okay, I'll go with you," she stammered, "Great. See you tomorrow, then. Sleep well," Thomas wished. "Thanks. You too," Isabella lay down on her bed.

On Saturday, the whole family went to a big basketball game. Isa was a fan of the round ball sport and had played herself before her illness. Thousands of visitors had come to see the Louisiana Dragons play the California All Stars and to cheer on their team. To their great delight, Annabelle and Thomas, her daughter's best friend, invited them to come along. The girls wore their jerseys and looked like cheerleaders themselves. When the game started, the crowd went wild. Isa was currently feeling good and healthy. Any examinations in the hospital and the therapy sessions went well. The mood in the hall was jovial and contagious. The whole family cheered along with the other fans. "You, Isa. Look who's sitting in front," Katy pointed in the finish line direction. Isabella's ex-boyfriend Jack also mingled with the basketball fans. However, not alone. His new girlfriend Hillary Spencer, was also there. The two held hands, kissed and watched the game together. "It's okay. I'm over it. At the end of the day, he wasn't the one for me," Isabella explained herself. "We're proud of you. This is our daughter," Thomas cheered. Jack and Hillary didn't hear about Isabella and her family. Isa was not interested in the topic any further. She focused on the game of her favorite team. The event was accompanied by music and dancing during the breaks. High house, the Louisiana Dragons won against the California All Stars. One of the professional basketball players signed autographs afterwards. Isabella and Katy picked up a personal autograph on their jersey. Their superstar Brian Mc Neil signed both their sports shirts and praised his fans. Totally moved, the girlfriends began to giggle. Isabella's attempt to stay cool didn't quite work. In the commotion, Isa noticed Jack and Hillary strolling hand in hand toward the exit. Inwardly, she said goodbye to him and was ready for her new and separate life. She had a great family and best friend by her side to support her. And newfound friends from Mississippi by now counted as well. An exciting family day was coming to an end.

Back at home, the twenty-year-old finished reading Ava's romance novel. She closed the book, a pleasant feeling of happiness coming over her. The novel ended as most readers would want it to. The happy ending that had been announced occurred. Now that she had finished reading, she brought the novel to her mother: "I finished reading. Ava is just the best. I'm curious to know what you think of the novel? I'm sure you'll love it!" Thankfully, Annabelle accepted the love story to read at a later hour. "Would you like to chop a salad with me? Vitamins ...", Annabelle wanted to continue conversation with her daughter. "I'd love to. But you chop the onions," Isabella grinned at her mother. She didn't mind and went about chopping the plant while her daughter chopped carrots and peppers. "You're doing really well right now. That's good to see," the ever-worried mother praised her heartbroken daughter. Thomas came home for dinner, still warm baguette bread and a bottle of wine for himself and his wife. A lit candle on the table was to give the dinner a cozy atmosphere. "Isa, we have something to tell you," the father introduced, looking into Isabella's questioning eyes. "Your mother and I have had a talk."

'What's coming now?' she was already anticipating new problems in her mind. Cheerful and pleased, the parents looked at their daughter. "The last time you were in Mississippi, it seemed to us that you came home with a renewed spirit." Isabella guessed the direction the conversation would take. 'Please let me drive,' she thought to herself, folding her hands unnoticed under the table. "If you want, we don't want to force you of course, then you may go there again? Of course, if it's okay with Ava? After all, the woman is already old," Thomas continued. "And how I want! Thank you a thousand times," Isa gleefully fell around her parents' necks. "I'll call Ava right now to clear this up," Isabella sprinted upstairs to her room to call Ava from her cell phone. What bliss; Ava was looking forward to Isabella's visit and agreed to arrive soon. "I'm allowed to come. She said yes," it poured out of her. She ran downstairs back to her parents. They were delighted with the positive confirmation from Mississippi. Even before she told Katy the great news, she texted Benjamin. He immediately called her cell phone. Again, hundreds of butterflies fluttered through Isabella's stomach as the cell phone rang. The news that Isabella's parents were suggesting the trip to Mississippi made Benjamin overjoyed and plunged him into anticipation. And the second piece of good news, that eighty-year-old Ava would welcome them into her home, made the young happiness shine. The last trip did Isabella's health good and the next one should be the same. "What are you packing? Take your most amazing and exciting clothes. Benjamin will be thrilled," Katy was blown away by the news surrounding Isabella. "He is the same way. No matter what I wear," the twenty-year-old was sure. "Then he's a good one. I'm so happy for you," the two friends indulged in each other's happiness anytime.

18.

Soon after, the trip was on the Greyhound bus to Mississippi for the second time. Her parents were sure that this trip would also do Isabella's heart good. Because there she was close again to her deceased heart donor Mary. Contact with Ava inspired their daughter, Thomas and Annabelle noted. And Benjamin seemed to be quite a nice young man, which pleased the parents as well. With little worry, the two let their daughter go. "Keep me posted. Am fully excited and have a good time!", Katy said goodbye to Isa. This time, too, the trip by long-distance bus went on for several hours. The joy of seeing Ava and Benji again was so great that Isabella would have loved to fly there to Mississippi just to be able to get there faster. She hoofed it and couldn't wait. What would she experience this time? In any case, she planned to borrow a second novel by the author to read. And she secretly hoped that Benjamin was planning another nice trip like the one he took to the Bienville National Forest. The bus ride seemed interminable to her. It was like she was visiting her second home. But she also realized that the trip only came about because Mary lost her life, and because of that fact, she had her still-healthy heart transplanted. Not nice, but true. Only this fate brought her together with Benjamin, his parents and Ava. Otherwise, she would most likely never have met her new friends. In the spirit of mindfulness and gratitude, she settled in for the long journey. At the bus stop, there was the first surprise. It was not Ava's neighbor who picked her up, but Benjamin with his parents. This had been agreed upon and was supposed to make Isabella happy. The greeting could not have been more friendly. Immediately, the young woman felt at home and arrived in the state of Mississippi. The sparkle in Isabella and Benjamin's eyes was hard for his parents to miss. The car ride brought Isa directly to Ava's house. 'Would the white, beautiful and magnificent building still stand as it did last time? And would the colorful flowers shine in the glow of the sun just as they did last time? And how was Ava, was she dressed as smartly again and carrying her head high with pride?' Question after question Isabella asked herself. Benji and she were both sitting in the back seat of his parents' car. They were smiling at each other and casting interested glances at each other. 'Does he look great again. And then he smells so good, too,' Isa gushed in her mind. The relationship with Jack was over and would not be resumed, she was sure of that. That's why she wasn't hurting anyone by flirting a little with Benjamin. Gradually they got closer to Ava's house until they finally reached it completely. There was a smell of meadows, fields and flowers everywhere. Lovely fragrance permeated through the open car window. Isabella saw Ava standing at the entrance of her house. She was wearing a green dress and had her hair elegantly pinned up. Matching earrings adorned her face. She had never seen such a pretty, fine eighty-year-old woman in all her life. The prestige and grace at first took Isabella's breath away. But she didn't want to let that show directly. Warmly, Isabella was welcomed by her hostess and the two quickly struck up a conversation. "I finished reading your novel. It's just great. My mom is reading it right now, too. That's why it's still in Louisiana," the young guest from the outstate explained. "I'm glad if you liked it. I hope your mom likes the story as much as you do?" Convinced, the ladies went upstairs. Ava had made Isabella's room incredibly beautiful and decorative once again. Fresh flowers from her front yard stood in a vase on the dresser. After Isa had freshened up and called her parents, she went downstairs to the others. They were already waiting for her visit. Benjamin's parents were also still there. The last time they visited, they wanted nothing to do with Isabella. The pain of losing Mary was still too deep in Benjamin's mother. She was not yet ready to meet the recipient of her sister's heart. Only when Isabella left again by bus did Benjamin's parents reconcile with her. They were all the more pleased to be there now. "Where are we going?", Isa wanted to know curiously. "To my sister's, if that's all right with you?" spoke Benji's mother, getting in the mood to visit the cemetery together.

With five people, they stood at Mary's grave. It was the second time for Isabella to visit the final resting place of her heart donor. At the cemetery, she felt a special connection to Mary. Benjamin's mother and

Ava both had bouquets of flowers with them. With great devotion, both women placed the bouquets on the grave of the deceased and Benji sang a little song of praise to his aunt. It was obvious even to strangers the deep sorrow that was in the hearts of Mary's family. She left a big hole. It wasn't something that could be filled quickly. Ava still didn't hire new household help; she generally found it hard to trust strangers. Finding a second Mary was never her intention and would be completely utopian for the octogenarian. With whom could she communicate so well, whom could she trust so blindly? Ava knew the answer herself: no one. Therefore, and because she couldn't finish her current novel anyway, she set about the housework herself. Even though it was difficult for her. A few women from the volunteer group Ava herself was a part of came to help her sporadically. She did not want to accept more help.

After the visit to the cemetery, everyone sat together at Ava's large dining table. Isabella, also Benjamin with his parents, and the hostess herself dined together as a family in the spirit of Mary. There was a fresh seafood platter consisting of various types of fish, crabs and mussels. Salad and garlic cream enhanced the menu. White wine and water were served with it. Isa had arrived in Mississippi only a few hours ago, but she already felt like a newborn. Late at night, Benjamin drove back home with his parents. Isabella slept as well in her guest room as if it had been her own bed. Because the next day was a Sunday, Benji got up early to see Isabella. After helping Ava in the kitchen in the morning after breakfast, she and Benjamin went outside to the garden. There, the two had some privacy and time to themselves. Benji asked Isabella interested questions about her heart condition. She explained to him that she suffered chronic myocarditis and had been hospitalized countless times because of it. Benjamin heard the term chronic myocarditis for the first time. When she nearly died, after a long wait, she received a heart transplant from his Aunt Mary. And she was to carry that inside her for the rest of her life. She explained all this to her crush. "You've been through a lot already. The fact that you're still so positive after all this speaks for you," Benji took Isabella's hand. Their affection for each other became more intimate, as did their conversations. Isabella felt like she had known Benjamin forever and trusted him unconditionally. She rarely felt as drawn to someone as she did to him. As a result, the young woman came clean. For hours Benjamin listened to her, she confided everything to him. Isa told about the family fate and the unsuccessful search for her grandmother. She told him about her breakup with Jack, who had already found a new flame in Hillary Spencer. And about the fact that she ended up in intensive care. She also told about her weekly hospital examinations and the therapy with Doctor Blum. She did not mince words and was not afraid to share her family's deepest secrets with Benjamin. She went on to say that she and her parents went to the adoption office together, but there was no information there about her grandmother. Finally she came to talk about the specialist lawyer, who would not find time again for another year. Thereupon hope and confidence left Annabelle. And Isa secretly concentrated on Internet research. Even on the World Wide Web, nothing could be found out. Last but not least, Isabella came up with the private detective who wanted to collect $5,000 in advance for his work. Money that she had been missing until now. "That was all. You're certainly shocked now, aren't you?" Isabella asked her listener after what felt like three hours. She couldn't believe he would still think she was great after all she had shared with him. But the worries proved to be unfounded. Benjamin thanked her in all seriousness for the information he confidently received from her. However, he did not inquire further. "Let's get up and go for a bike ride. Like we did the other day," he suggested to the twenty-year-old. Isabella looked around questioningly for bicycles. There was grass and flowers growing in Ava's yard, but no bikes to ride. "In Ava's shed, my parents and I put two bikes a few days ago. They're from our house," Benjamin was well prepared. Isabella couldn't have imagined anything better, she was insanely happy. After they had packed provisions, the two also cycled off. For the rest of the day, they rode freely and in high spirits through the beautiful area where Ava lived. The warm weather invited them to linger and rest in the fields. The young people lay down on the ground of the field, protected and unobserved by a lot of corn. And again she was invited to lie in Benjamin's arm. The world could have stood still for both souls in the cornfield. Together they lay there in silence and sometimes talking. Here she wanted to stay and never get up again. Then Isabella praised the novel she had read by the writer Ava. "I really liked the romance novel. My mum is reading it herself right now. Am already looking forward to the next novel I will read by Ava. She has written, I think, 50 romance novels already. Funny I've never heard of her before. But then, she avoids the public and the press, so that's obvious. She does her work in the privacy of her own home." Benjamin could only remain silent about this. Isa suspected that she had shocked him with too much information earlier. He certainly didn't want a girlfriend with a lot of drama. The unfulfilled wish to meet the grandmother, then she almost died, the heart transplant ... Isabella figured that Benjamin's silence had to do with her and all the information around her. She firmly believed that he would distance himself from her. "I can understand your silence. And honestly, I shouldn't have told you my whole life story. You just seem so familiar to me. I apologize. I can understand if this is all too much for you." The young man remained silent and thought. 'Now say something, please. I can't stand it otherwise,' Isa talked to herself. The seconds passed, it became increasingly burdensome for the woman who revealed herself completely earlier. She could already see herself sitting on the next bus home. Then, finally, Benji broke his silence. "That you women always think it has everything to do with you right away. I have to disappoint you. Even though you told me a lot, it has nothing to do with you right now," he explained. "Who does it have anything to do with?", Isabella wants to know without being put off. Benji thought for a moment before answering, "You were just talking about Ava and her novel..." he paused again. Isa was getting more and more impatient. "Right. I think her novel is great and I want to read the next one soon." Benjamin looked at the floor, talking more slowly, and it seemed as if he were involved. "That's just the point. On the face of it, her novels are terrific. An old woman with class and style; a world-famous writer." Isabella nodded, agreeing. She just didn't understand what this was supposed to be about? Benji became more specific in his comments, "How should I put this? There have been problems with Ava for some time." Benjamin slowly raised his head, looking at his conversation partner. She was completely puzzled and irritated. "What do you mean? Problems with Ava? I can't imagine that at all. She seems so perfect. Do you have arguments with her or your parents?" Ava was a born perfectionist for Isabella and a role model in many ways. "No, I don't mean it that way. We don't have a fight with her. I've never known anyone to have a fight with her," the 25-year-old explained. "Today you trusted me with everything. Now I trust you, can you do that Isabella?", with a serious expression he looked her in the eyes and continued. "Ava can't write anymore. For a long time now ..." Isabella began to laugh. "What do you mean she can't write anymore? Did she sprain her finger? Ah, okay. She can't write anymore because she's just gotten too old. I mean, who writes romantic romance novels at 80 these days?" For Isa, that seemed to be the only valid reason. She poked a little fun at Benjamin's remarks. But she was wrong. "No, it isn't. I know her. There's something else behind it. For her age, Ava is physically and cognitively fine." Benji seemed more interested in the matter than Isabella had previously assumed. Ava was very important to him. "I believe you know her well. But she doesn't have to tell you everything, after all. Maybe she has an illness and is just keeping quiet about it because she doesn't want to be a burden to anyone. Her not hiring a new housekeeper, after Mary's death, may have to do with shame about her age and a possible illness. I'm sure she doesn't want anyone to know. Not even you," Isabella rhymed and speculated in her imagination. Benjamin pulled down his cap and shook his head. He didn't want to believe what Isabella feared. Perplexed, he propped his head up with his right hand. "Isa, please believe me. I know her long and well. She has no illness. And she is not ashamed either. She liked my aunt very much, she misses Mary like we all do. That's why she hasn't hired anyone new yet. She owns a big house and leaves some manuscripts lying around the office. Trust is generally hard for her." Isabella did not take Benjamin's concern seriously, to his regret. For her, something was important if it was an emergency, such as a heart transplant or a terrible accident. "You know what's funny?" again he looked at Isa, bitterly serious and apprehensive. "Ava, our friend of eighty years, fifty in number she has written. Fifty novels are solely her work. And they are always structured in the same way: they are about two people who love each other, drama, and a happy ending at the end. Fifty times always the same. She has never changed course. And tell me Isabella, what is part of love?"

The twenty-year-old had been shaped by her illness with a lot of life experience. What belonged to love for her was clear. "Well. For me, love includes: dating, falling in love, moving in together, trusting each other, marriage, children ...", Isabella enumerated. Then she was interrupted. "That's just it. You said it: children. Whether you believe me or not? There is never a single child in any of her 50 novels. Isn't that funny? After all, if two people love each other, they're going to want to have a child at some point, or am I wrong? In no story does she mention that any of the characters in her books have a child or that there is a patchwork family. That nephews, nieces or grandchildren exist. Not once at the end of the story do the lovers have a child. You can read them all, I did. Out of fifty books, there are zero that have a child in them. And don't tell me Ava is a modern woman and she didn't mention children because of female emancipation. She's 80 years old, after all." Benjamin talked himself into a frenzy.

Isabella slowly understood what he was about and she noticed how important Ava was to him. Benji paused talking and took a bottle of water from his backpack. He had gotten so carried away with his questions around the writer that he was getting warm and starting to sweat. They both shared the bottle of water and continued to think. "For weeks, it could be months, she's been sitting on her 51st novel and has writer's block. She's never had that before. She can't get the novel finished and I wonder why? Sometimes I would watch her unobtrusively. She would sit at her desk and I could literally feel her despair. Something was bothering her. Ava would put the pen down and then put it down again, staring into space. At some point, she stopped writing at all. There's something wrong. I want to know why she can't finish the 51st novel?" Benjamin looked thoughtful and also desperate. Since Isabella liked him very much, she took his hand and held it tightly. "You listened to me and I listened to you. That's what friends do." Benjamin smiled at his confidante; they had become really good friends after a short time. Benji's hunch was that Ava was carrying a secret. Together, the two decided that they would solve the mystery of Ava. It would then remain their shared secret. Isabella was already experiencing her time in Mississippi as exciting and full of adventure. She had only just arrived. The fact that they wanted to find out something about Ava also meant that she would spend more time with Benjamin. Which, of course, pleased her very much. Benji suggested looking for clues at Ava's house when she would be invited back to a charity meeting. With the bikes and their secret in their luggage, the two drove back to the house. Isabella found it difficult to keep a low profile. After what Benji had said to her, she had to think about her hostess much more than before. She could no longer look her directly in the eye. "How was your bike ride? Did you have fun?" the octogenarian wanted to know from Isabella. Somewhat distracted by thoughts surrounding the question of why her novels have been childless so far, Isabella replied, "Yes, it was really very nice. Great neighborhood here. And I'm glad I can get back out into nature after my hospital stays. Thank you Ava for letting me be your guest here." Isa just barely got her act together. Ava was touched by the kind words and put her hand on Isabella's shoulder. "You are welcome in my house anytime," Ava replied to the thank you note. Isa felt guilty, because she and Benjamin had finally planned to search Ava's house for possible clues. And this after the hostess had just offered her eternal welcome. In between the two women's conversation, Benji slipped into the kitchen to look at Ava's calendar. Quietly, he cheered because the calendar showed a charity meeting for Ava in two days. In the living room, he flashed his index and middle fingers up, which was supposed to mean two. Isa figured what was meant by that as she continued to talk with Ava. For the next day and a half, Isabella tried to find out information about her hostess without being noticed. She felt like a spy or an agent. Her talent for obtaining information about someone had so far largely failed. After all, she was not getting any useful information about her missing grandmother in the world of the Internet. Now she was playing private detective herself. Benjamin was her colleague and only ally in this game. Then, finally, the time had come. Ava came down the stairs smartly dressed and said goodbye to Isabella for a few hours. "If anything comes up, you can always call me at the charity center. The number is on the kitchen table." Outside, a car was already honking to take Ava to the meeting. Benjamin and Isa now had free rein to snoop around Ava's property for several hours. Sometimes in pairs, sometimes separately, the two searched the huge house for clues to Ava's problems. "You look in the bedroom and bathroom. I'll look on the first floor," Benjamin voiced his plan. He would look everywhere, but Ava's bedroom was off limits to him. His respect for the old lady was too great. Because Isabella is also a woman, this should be easier for her. All the rooms were scrutinized and every object, no matter how suspicious, was looked at in detail. "I hope she doesn't come back soon already. Otherwise it was all for nothing if we haven't found anything by then," Benji spoke in a slight panic. Then the two ended up in the writer's writing room. "Remember. We can't let her know we've been snooping around. We have to put everything down exactly as it was lying before," Benjamin considered every detail and took the role of leader in the search. "Yes, sir," Isabella joked. There was quite a bit of paperwork and different colored pens on the desk. It was difficult to search accurately while leaving everything as it was before. The cupboards and dressers were inspected by private detective Benjamin. He left nothing out and even looked behind the curtains. Isabella studied some of the writer's files to get information about her. She felt a little strange about it, but she knew she would never want to harm Ava. The adrenaline was building in her body, it felt more like a game to her. A game that would quickly turn serious. "What can the key be for?", Benji immediately took the small key his accomplice had just found in the wooden pen holder on Ava's desk. "That's what we have to find out. Let's hurry before she comes back," the team searched all over the octogenarian's office. "Look at that box up there on top of the cabinet," sleuth Isa spotted. "You are the best. It's sure to fit on there. Come on, let's get the box down," he stood on a chair and handed the mysterious box to his girlfriend. With trembling hands, Isabella put the small key into the lock of the chest. "It turns. It's a miracle," Isa and Benji looked expectantly at the chest. Slowly, she opened the chest until the undiscovered was revealed. Benjamin kept his mouth open in excitement. He was amazed and gobsmacked at the same time after so long. Looking for a clue was definitely worth it for him. Isabella, on the other hand, stood distraught and confused in Ava's office. "We found it!" the excited young man shouted out loud. Isabella still stood by, startled and wordless.

"What do you have?", Benjamin couldn't understand why Isabella's joy was so clouded? The young woman held the contents of the box in her hand.

Half a heart carved out of wood.

Shocked and in a depressed mood, she said in a low tone, "My mother has one just like it lying in a hidden box at home. I discovered it when I was a child."

Now Benjamin was speechless. "May I hold the heart?" he asked unobtrusively. Isa timidly handed him half the wooden heart. "It looks like it was carved by myself. I'm sure it's old. Are you sure your mother has one like it? Could have bought one somewhere back then?" Benji asked critical questions first. He did not yet see a connection between Ava and Isabella's mother.

"My mother's looks the same. I remember that very well. She has the other half. I'm sure she does," without a doubt Isabella briskly ran to her guest room and put the half heart in her suitcase. Quickly, the two set up the writing room as it looked before. They placed the case and the small key in their respective places and headed downstairs to the living room, not wanting to talk about it any further. Ava returned from her meeting a short time later and told the young people about the conversations at the charity center. Benji then said goodbye to start his way home. For Isabella, the coming night remained sleepless. The found half heart did not let her go mentally.

Accordingly, she was tired the next day. Isa was even less able to look Ava in the eye at breakfast than before. In addition, she yawned most of the time. The plan to search everything in her house for clues made the young woman feel guilty. And the success of having found a clue could not have been more bizarre for Isabella. Half a heart carved out of wood, enclosed in a box. Her mother had one just like it. What this was supposed to mean boggled Isabella's mind. It meant that she could no longer look the octogenarian in the face. How should she react to Ava and how should she talk to her? Isa had never been good at keeping secrets all her life. This task was difficult for her and she hoped to get an answer to the hidden wooden heart soon. In this case, the fact that she had to leave again came as a convenient surprise to the twenty-year-old. She was getting nowhere with her research in the state of Mississippi for the time being and knew what task was waiting for her back home in Louisiana. To find the other half and find out what secret was kept with it. This was the next step. "Isabella, I hope you find out what this is all about back in Louisiana? Please call me and keep me posted. If only for your health," Benjamin expressed his sincere interest in Isabella. She packed her suitcase in the guest room and took the precaution of checking whether the wooden heart was still in it? 'Phew, luckily still there,' she thought to herself. Benji was about to carry the suitcase downstairs when he stopped at the room door. 'I haven't forgotten anything, my suitcase is completely packed,' Isabella griped beforehand. Benjamin was of the opinion that she had forgotten something after all. "We both forgot something," he answered her and kissed her tenderly on the mouth. Isabella was blown away, she naturally returned the romantic kiss. Both smiled at each other, it was clear to them that they liked each other very much and should not have seen the last time. "Well, now I have to go. Otherwise I'll miss the bus," Isa had to say, although she would have liked to keep kissing Benjamin. The two hurried down the stairs with their packed suitcases. Benjamin's parents took the visitor back to the long-distance bus stop. The Greyhound was already standing in its position, ready to depart. Ava, who fortunately didn't notice the missing wooden heart, and the enamored Benjamin were also there. "Nice to have met you. Hopefully you'll come back to visit sometime? Because my son thinks a lot of you," Benjamin's mother spoke without mincing words. "Mum. That's all right now," Benji said awkwardly, but also with a smile toward his mother. Isabella politely shook hands with Benjamin's parents in farewell. Then she stood in front of Ava, suddenly not knowing what to do? "It was very nice with you again. Come home well and see you soon dear Isabella," Ava, who rarely showed emotion, told the twenty-year-old how much she appreciated her presence. "See you soon dear Ava," Isabella replied, finally looking the old lady in the eyes again. In front of the three elderly people present, Benjamin quickly kissed his Isabella goodbye on the mouth before she boarded the bus.

The two felt a little shame, but Benjamin was already 25 years old and Isabella 20. Accordingly, they did not need to be ashamed of their feelings. Isa kissed her heart donor's nephew on the mouth. She seemed to be connected to Mary's family, on one side and on the other.

The bus flashed its lights and departed, Isabella waving to her new friends from the bus. She knew this was not goodbye forever. During the ride, she pondered the connection between Ava's half-wooden heart and her mother Annabelle's. The destination of the long journey was her home in Louisiana, where she was warmly welcomed by her family.

19.

Isabella had no intention of looking for the other half right away. She wanted to keep open the possibility of tracking it down when she felt like it. Besides, there was the unpalatable possibility that the heart she was looking for was no longer hidden in the box where Isabella once found it as a child. Sometimes she even wondered to herself if she had imagined the heart in the box? The hope that that heart was still there should be maintained as long as possible. And if it was a dream, then this would have been the most beautiful dream forever.

For this reason, she wanted to get used to her home in Louisiana again first and then distracted herself with her everyday life. She was so focused on forgetting about the heart that she became more and more subjected to the stress of everyday life. She was doing well physically. From there, she did not notice the negative effects the stress was causing her. The weekly therapy session and hospital check-ups continued consistently. So did the yoga training and walking in the open air. Every day, her best friend Katy came over to chat. Although Isabella liked her a lot, she didn't tell Katy about Benjamin's suspicions about Ava. And certainly nothing about the key that opened the box containing half the heart made of wood. And about the fact that Isa thought that her mother had also hidden such a self-carved half heart of wood in a box. Isabella told nothing of all this. And that, although she had known Katy all her life. She only confided in her best friend that she had a good time in Mississippi and that Benjamin kissed her lovingly on the mouth. Katy, on the other hand, ran story after story about her male classmates, college, the bitches in her major, and from work. In the evenings, Isa and her parents sat together at the table and played Scrabble. Or they would watch a show on TV together and help themselves to the Chinese food they ordered once a week. She had gradually returned home. Every day she answered letters from other friends. Young women with whom she had gone to school and played sports. She didn't write with Ava yet, first she had to find out if the other heart had been just a dream or really existed? Benjamin, on the other hand, called every day and wanted to know if she had started looking? And, of course, if she had fared well? To Isabella's delight, Benji informed her that he missed her at all times. These were the good things in the young woman's daily life. Increasingly, she stressed herself with the thought of what she could work or study soon? The heart transplant was successful and the follow-up examinations in the hospital were promising for a healthy future. But what did she trust herself to do and would she want to do? What were her body, heart and immune system up to? Could she manage to study or go to work full time? Which study or work would that be? One thing was clear: she could not and must not pursue high-performance sports ever again in her life. Many questions came to her mind, and Isabella's head was buzzing. It was all getting to be too much. Annabelle and Thomas urged their daughter to pursue part-time studies. A possible scholarship was offered by an organization for patients with heart disease, of which Isabella was one. "They personally offer you the opportunity to go to college here in Louisiana. That means you could stay with us. During the semester break, of course, you'd be allowed to go to Mississippi. And the good thing is, you're not required to join a sports team because of your condition. Doesn't that sound great?" Annabelle and Thomas were bright-eyed about their daughter's future. "It would be a waste of your talents if you didn't study," her father added, "This is a once-in-a-lifetime opportunity."

Isabella was going way too fast, thinking what was she going to do with her life?

Spontaneously, she replied, "I'm not sure I want to study? Maybe I'll just do something good or at least belong to a good cause." Her parents were not entirely convinced by their daughter's ideas. "If you study, then you can join a lot of good organizations. Or you go into politics? Issues you stand up for; then you fight for them. Isabella, you've proven to everyone what a great fighter you are. And that you have something to say. Don't waste your voice. Or you can help with volunteer projects," her father's speech sounded like a political campaign speech. Her head was spinning. She didn't have a plan for the future yet, except that one day she wanted to do something good for the community. Visibly overwhelmed and exhausted, she called for calm: "I can't and don't want to decide yet. If I commit myself to something specific, then that is a far-reaching decision for the future. And then I live according to that. I have to think about it and clear my head." Even if it wasn't what her parents wanted to hear, it was still a concrete answer. The decision was up to Isabella herself. On bike rides in Mississippi, she always felt free and carefree. In Louisiana, she hadn't ridden a bike in ages. She needed to get out of her home. All alone, she rode the train far out of town. In a rural setting, she got off and walked to a nearby park where she rented a bike. Even though it was without Benjamin, Isabella felt free as a bird on the borrowed yellow wire bike. After a while, she stopped the bike and lay down on the grass. She closed her eyes and went deep inside herself. Isa grabbed her heart and started talking to Mary, "You are so close to me and yet so far. Can you tell me what I should do? Study or go to work? I'm sure you would have had an answer. Doing good for other people pleases me too. It's hard to please everyone. My parents want me to study. I'm sure your nephew would like to get to know me better and see me more often. That is also my interest. I'm caught in the middle and don't know what I'm called to do? Oh Mary, if you can, please give me an answer."

The desired solution was not immediately forthcoming this time either. Isabella noticed that she was getting further and further away from the actual topic. And was making life difficult for herself by distracting herself. The big topic in Mississippi was and remained the found half heart. What was the matter with it now? The young woman realized she had to face the truth. Constantly running away would only make things worse. She had suppressed what she was actually looking for. 'If I don't know anything else either. That way I know I'll be looking for the heart tomorrow when Dad's at work and Mum's at the dentist.' Full of vigor and zest for action, the twenty-year-old returned the borrowed yellow bike and took the train back home. Thomas and Annabelle were glad that their daughter had not run away again, but had come home in good shape.

The next day dawned and rarely did the young fighter feverishly anticipate a doctor's appointment for her mother like this one at the dentist. "I'll see you later honey. In the meantime, you can think about what major you're interested in?" Annabelle could already see her daughter studying on campus as she once had. "No mother. I'm thinking now where is your wooden heart?" whispered Isabella softly as her mother made her way out the door to head to the dentist. 'It's now or never,' Isa thought to herself and went up to the attic of the house. It had seemed so creepy to her even as a child. And yet she often went up there to play treasure hunt. She felt like a gold digger today. "Where have you been hiding?" Isa looked for the box where she thought the heart was. Since the whole attic was full of boxes, cartons, lots of junk and full of dust, she had a hard time searching at first. The air in the attic was dusty and stuffy. "Seek and you shall find. This could be the box," Isa talked to herself a little. Well hidden in the attic, she discovered an old dusty chest. Childhood memories came back to her and she felt that this could be the box she was looking for. She had discovered and opened it as a child, so it couldn't have been a dream. It felt real. As if in a magical moment, she slowly and gently opened the lid of the dusty chest. It squeaked a bit when she opened it because it had been sitting on top for years without being permanently opened. Her faint memories had not failed her. It was not a dream, because the contents of this chest matched the contents of Ava's chest.

The other half of the carved wooden heart was in Annabelle's box.

The half heart had been secretly hidden in a box up in the attic for years, if not decades. She was not mistaken, the heart really existed.

But what did it mean? Was there a connection? Isabella seemed at first still perplexed, but also overwhelmed by the events.

Would the two halves fit into each other and belong together?

She took the finely carved half heart and left the attic as she found it. Once her parents would be present, she planned to broach the subject gently. Annabelle planned to go shopping after the dentist appointment. Then she would come home at about the same time as Thomas. Soon it should be that time. Quickly picking up the phone, Isabella dialed Benjamin's number in Mississippi and told him about the miracle she was experiencing. Benji could hardly believe it himself and asked her to send a photo of half the heart via cell phone. When he caught sight of the other half via his cell phone screen, he was stunned. "It really looks like the half heart from Ava's office. Have you held both halves together yet?" he wanted to know with curiosity. "No. I haven't had time yet. You, I think my parents just got home. I'm hanging up now," Isabella said goodbye to Benjamin. "Good luck," he still called into the receiver, but he was too slow. Isabella had already hung up. Running down the stairs, Isa didn't care at all this time to wait for the right moment. Because there never would be. In the past, she often tried to wait for the ideal moment when addressing difficult topics. But unfortunately without success. That's why she didn't want to wait so long this time and address the unloved topic more quickly. Annabelle and Thomas were talking in the kitchen about the dentist appointment and were about to start cooking. A little small talk ensued.

Thomas told about a discussion at work he had with an unconvincing driver. His wife told about her unpopular root canal treatment and the subsequent shopping in the supermarket, where she met annoying and talkative people, in whose conversation she did not want to get involved. Her stomach growled, she just wanted to cook quickly, eat and then rest. It had been two hours since her visit to the dentist and she was now allowed to eat something nutritious. She did not count on her daughter today. Isa was nervous inside as she had rarely been before. Her heart was beating too fast, which was not good for her. But she intended to get it over with quickly and talk to her mother. She had one half of Annabelle with her. The other half of Ava was still hidden upstairs. "What have you got under your T-shirt?" her mum wanted to know. 'Eyes closed and through,' the twenty-year-old thought to herself and pulled out the half heart made of wood from under her T-shirt. Her mom cringed at the sight as if she had seen a ghost or a burglar just trying to break into her house. "Where did you get that?" she asked nervously. Slightly belligerent, Isabella answered straightforwardly, "I had found this up in the attic when I was a kid. Now I went all the way back upstairs to see if it was still there? It wasn't a dream, this heart really exists." Her father, Thomas, immediately stepped in. "Give it to me, please!" he commanded her in one short sentence. Isabella found her parents' behavior funny and didn't let up. "Why? What's wrong with it?" Annabelle stood in the kitchen with tears in her eyes, speechless at first. "It's very important to me. Give it to me, please," her mother's face rarely contorted as much as it did at that moment. "I just want to know what about it?", Isa became defiant, "Where did you get it? And from whom? It's been hidden upstairs for a long time." The line seemed to be slowly crossed. "It's none of your business." Annabelle grew louder and raised her voice. "I just want to know where you got it?" Now her father sparked in, feeling compelled to end the line of questioning. "That's enough Isabella. Is enough for today," he took half the heart out of her hand, so fast the young woman could not look. A skilful move as a policeman, after all. The young fighter wouldn't stop asking. "You could pass well as a cop. Ever thought of that?" now her father was getting a little ironic and snarky. While father and daughter were engaged in a discussion of principles, a muffled sound suddenly opened up. Annabelle had collapsed. "Oh, my God," her husband cried, immediately rushing over to his wife. "Call the ambulance, now!", Isabella followed her father's instructions and hurriedly picked up the phone to dial 911. Her conscience could not have been worse. Isabella had tears running down her face from shame, embarrassment and sadness. What had she done to her mother? 'Mum fainted because of me. It's my fault. Only and only me. Why didn't I stop asking?' a thousand thoughts raced through her head. "Mum, hang in there. Please!", she stroked her mother's hair and face, who was still lying unconscious on the floor. The last few times, and for most of her life, Isabella had been the one admitted to the hospital. Today was going to be different. A short time later, emergency services arrived at her house. The emergency doctor began the first medical measures, while a paramedic pushed the stretcher into the ambulance. With blue lights flashing, the car drove to the nearest hospital. Thomas and Isabella followed in the family car. The two remained silent during the car ride. Only the tears on Isabella's cheeks spoke for themselves. At the hospital, Mother Annabelle was immediately given a thorough examination. "Can you explain the reason for your wife's sudden fainting? Has anything out of the ordinary happened to you in the last few hours?" the doctor was alert and asked the right questions in the right place. "Well. There was an argument at our house. It was between my wife and my daughter. My daughter wouldn't let up, she kept bringing up a subject, which didn't sit well with my wife," Thomas explained to the attending physician. Isa felt the looks from the doctor, that's why her face blushed. And she was ashamed to the core, most of all of herself. 'What have I done? I can never make it up to you,' Isabella was plagued by heavy, self-imposed reproaches. Her father, for whom she was still the little princess, looked at her with contempt. At least, it seemed that way to her. It was clear to Isa that her father had no real hatred for her, but he loved his wife very much and was now very worried about her. "There's another woman from our family in the hospital today," he tried to joke with a familiar nurse. "Oh, they take turns with them?" the orderly asked, slightly ironically. Time passed for a while until Thomas sat down with his daughter. "She has to stay here. We can't do anything for her now. We'll go back tomorrow," in a clouded voice, he told his daughter about the conversation with the doctor. Once home, father and daughter had lost their appetites. Isabella agonizingly retreated to her room. On her cell phone, she looked at photos of her mother. Highly emotional, she crawled into the valley of tears. Then she called Benjamin in Mississippi. He was the only one who knew the argument was about the two halves of hearts. Benji never would have guessed that the conversation between the two women would turn out this way. Somehow he felt partly responsible for the circumstances in which Isabella's mother found herself at the moment. Isabella wrote a letter to Ava simply to say that her mother had collapsed and was now in the hospital. She did not mention anything in the letter about the circumstances and how it happened. Isa herself was deeply affected and not well, she told Ava in the short letter. She said the same thing to her best friend Katy on the phone. Simply that Annabelle had fainted and now had to stay in the hospital. Other than that, the twenty-year-old kept a very low profile with information around what triggered her mother's collapse. She had already caused enough trouble in the past, at least that was how she felt herself. Half the night she looked at old photo albums from her childhood. In many photos she was smiling with her mother in her arms. Annabelle's love accompanied her through her life and strengthened her in her illness. Isabella owed everything to her mother. She knew that her mum grew up without her biological mother and still suffered from it today. Even though she constantly declared it closed. She continued to look closely at each family photo in loving memory until she eventually fell asleep among the albums.

The next day, Thomas and Isabella visited their beloved in the hospital. A large bouquet of flowers could not be missing, of course. The doctor took Thomas to his side beforehand, while Isa stood by and listened. "Your wife needs rest now, lots of rest. We'll leave her here for a few days for observation," the doctor shared further. "What's wrong with her? Were they able to find anything specific?", Thomas was eager to know. "She most likely fainted due to stress and an altercation at their home. Possibly it could be that, because her blood values and the examinations were fine as far as I could determine," the doctor gave the all-clear at least on these points. Thomas thanked him for the information and went with his daughter to Annabelle's hospital room. The couple greeted each other full of love and fulfilled affection, the sight could not have been more beautiful for their daughter Isabella. Annabelle gratefully accepted the flowers. Now Isa had to turn herself in. With a little fear of her mother's reaction, she stood next to the hospital bed and met her with a touching look. "I'm so sorry, Mum. I wish I could undo it. And I'm ashamed of my behavior," Isabelle's apology sounded sincere and was unceremoniously accepted by her mother. Annabelle was still a little weak, the last few months had not passed her by without leaving a trace. "You are my child and always will be," she replied, taking her daughter's hand. Should probably mean as much as apology accepted. The two women embraced and it seemed that everything was going to be all right again. Thomas was pleased with the situation and hoped for a calmer future in his house.

All of a sudden the door opened. Katy along with her parents were standing in Annabelle's room. "What are you doing here?" the patient wanted to know. "We wanted to check on you and all of you. Your daughter had called Katy and told her you had fainted. That's why we're here. And we wanted to ask if you needed help with anything? I guess Isabella wasn't feeling as well as Katy said either," Katy's mother shared. Annabelle had not expected such care and helpfulness. Katy's family's interest in Isabella's family was sincere. Isabella's best friend also presented Annabelle with a bouquet of flowers. The family stayed to visit for a few hours, and in the evening they said goodbye again. "Thank you for being there. And if we need help, we'll let you know," Thomas was overwhelmed by this friendship. To support each other in such a way touched the policeman anew. The day ended with a good feeling for everyone. Isabella's family reconciled peacefully, and they had the support of Katy's family. A comforting and grateful feeling returned to Isabella. The very next day, new events were to enter the life around Isabella's family. Thomas and his daughter came to the hospital again for a visit. Annabelle made a solid impression and gave no reason for further concern. Fresh wind moved into the hospital and brought a lot of news. There were actually two people from Mississippi standing in the hallway of the infirmary inquiring which room Annabelle would be in? Isa felt inside that something was about to change. But she did not yet know what? When knocking on Annabelle's room door, Isabella's heart beat excitedly and fast. Something was about to happen. Ava and Benjamin entered the door. "I don't think so. What are you guys doing here in Louisiana? And then at the hospital. Is this a dream?" Isa immediately realized that this was not a dream. Truly, the two were standing before her. Isabella hugged her guests effusively. "Mom, Dad, these are my friends from Mississippi. Benjamin, the nephew of my heart donor Mary. And Ava, she's where Benji's aunt worked and was a particularly good friend of Mary's. I used to spend the night at her place, as you know," Isabella introduced each person. Friendly, they shook hands in greeting. "It's nice that you came all the way here to visit us. Unfortunately, I have to pass right now. Stuck here," Annabelle grinned and smirked. "We don't want to inconvenience them. Isabella's been to see us in Mississippi twice before. And when she called and wrote us that she was in the hospital and that she herself wasn't feeling well, we thought it was time to come to Louisiana ourselves. She had always supported me when she was our guest in Mississippi. And now it seemed to us that her daughter needed help," Ava said, explaining the visit. Benjamin and Isabella smiled at each other and embraced. Benji also presented a lavish bouquet of flowers to Annabelle. The hospital room had been transformed into a sea of flowers, glowing with all colors. "We also went on the Greyhound. And checked into the hotel near your house," Benjamin was happy to see Isabella again and took her by the hand. "Well, then. Welcome to Louisiana and to our family," Thomas greeted the two newcomers. The newly in love young people unceremoniously retreated to a quiet corner of the hospital. Benjamin took the initiative and kissed his Isabella on the mouth again. At that moment, she could not have been happier. The two decided that they would now officially be a couple. The long distance should not be an obstacle for the love of the two. Overjoyed and filled with endorphins, they strolled through the hospital hand in hand. "Are you brave?", Benji asked his girlfriend, "Mostly. Why?" she wanted to know. "Do you purely happen to have the two halves with you?" the young man continued to ask brashly and daringly. "Purely by chance yes," Isa and her friend made a risky and daring plan. Would it work out, as they imagined? The two themselves did not know what was behind the story about the two hearts? When the two of them came back into the hospital room, hand in hand and beaming happily, all three adults realized that the two of them belonged together from now on. Thomas liked Benjamin right away and was okay with the relationship. Ava and Isabella's parents were having tea when Isa determinedly and fearlessly set something in motion. What she would do with it, she did not know at that minute? The due date had come and it was to change her life in a relevant way.

Isabella took out one half of the heart from her pocket and placed it on the side table by her mother's bedside. Benjamin watched the situation closely. Annabelle and Thomas watched and could do nothing. Eighty-year-old Ava was about to collapse when she noticed the heart.

"Why did you take my heart away, Isabella?" the old lady wanted to know.

"It's not yours. This one is from my mother, Annabelle. She had it hidden in a box in the attic. I still have yours in my bag," Benjamin handed his girlfriend the shoulder bag.

Isabella took out the other half and brought both hearts together.

Two halves became one whole.

Under the meticulous observation of the four people present, the joined heart now stood on the side table.

Ava toppled over.

20.

Thomas immediately ran to the octogenarian. Benjamin also made himself useful by calling a doctor as quickly as possible. Annabelle, meanwhile, looked at her daughter questioningly. The nurses and the doctor led Ava away to examine her. "What's the meaning of this?" asked Annabelle of her daughter as Ava left the room. "Well, what do you think? I think we know now," Isa looked at her mother's puzzled face. The latter remained silent from then on, thinking. After the examination, Ava was placed on the hospital bed next to Annabelle. "We had considered putting her in another room. She also keeled over due to a stressful situation that obviously happened in this room. After all, that seems to happen a lot in her family. Keep in mind that the lady is already 80 years old and needs rest. If the lady doesn't find rest, we will have to move her," the otherwise so nice doctor suddenly didn't act so nice anymore. Annabelle and Thomas looked at each other sheepishly. Ava was hooked up to the drip so that her body would get enough fluids. Slowly her consciousness returned and she opened her eyes. Isabella, Benjamin and Thomas stood around the eighty-year-old woman, eager to attend. "I wouldn't have thought that a few hours ago. That I'm lying next to them now," Ava joked, still slightly dazed, toward Annabelle, who was most sorry about the whole situation. The old woman had come all the way from

Mississippi, had been there for less than two hours, and was already confronted with a difficult topic that she had not been able to anticipate beforehand.

"I want to tell you something," Ava said. All eyes were on her. Annabelle was almost breathless and Isabella was eagerly waiting for this moment. She was already expecting something to follow, something to do with the two hearts. "They don't have to tell anything if it doesn't make them feel good," Thomas intervened protectively. Isa would have preferred to interrupt her father, because it seemed like the usually secretive Ava wanted to come clean. "It's all right. I think it's time to tell now..."

So she lay next to Annabelle on her hospital bed, the headboard raised so she could sit upright and tell. Isabella, Benjamin and Thomas sat around Ava and Annabelle. As if they were a closed circle. Tense and with great expectations they listened to the words of the old lady.

"Well, that was so ...", Ava began to tell her story.

Mississippi 1946

When the war was over, my private schooling was completed at home. I was finally able to attend elementary school.

Later, in 1951, I was sent by my parents to a boarding school for girls. I was to enjoy the best school education. The first time I just cried and wanted to go home. But I stayed there with the aim to get the highest school degree. Everything was so stiff and strict. I only felt comfortable there years later. Some of the other girls and young women were too conniving and arrogant for me. Daughters from the richest and most respected families in America, daughters of politicians and millionaires. Everyone with rank and name from the southern states was supposed to bring their daughter to this elite boarding school. My childhood and adolescence passed with me wanting to write stories and being forbidden to do so by every adult around me. Everything I experienced I processed in my stories, which I rewrote in such a way that not everyone understood it right away. I transformed nasty and unloved people into animal creatures. Bad situations were immersed in magical worlds. But some teachers and professors were highly intelligent, culturally educated and luminaries in their field in interpreting literature. To my parents, especially my father, my writing was just shame and ridiculous kid stuff. They didn't take me seriously and never told anyone how much I enjoyed trying to express myself in writing. "We'll have to beat that out of her. People will have a good laugh at her. Our reputation is at risk with this," my father wanted to forbid me from writing any more stories. A fine young lady from a respectable house would not do such a thing. For me, playing the cello, gymnastics and, first and foremost, learning were the order of the day. I was to become something, and it was a matter of course for my father that I should marry later in a manner befitting my station and bring children into the world, preferably three boys. When my ambiguous stories got out of hand one day, my parents were summoned to the office of the professor of literature. "Your daughter is exceptionally gifted. You have to give her that. However, in the wrong field, I tend to think. You certainly don't want your daughter to become the next Gertrude Stein!" professor Dr. Dr. Philipps warned my parents. "We amuse and ignore such people," my father dismissed the writer and art collector. My mother did not form her own opinion. Rather, her opinion was the same as my father's. Hard as a rock, cold and unfeeling, people called her. One father was the top director of a large bank. The biggest in Mississippi. He was known for his hard hand and his will to run a business. I think that his employees suffered under him. He did not know pity. The richer a customer was, the higher the chance that my father would leave his office to stride down the marble stairs to observe the male customer, what business he was doing in the bank, and what he looked like. Only when my father knew this did he go back upstairs to his office. If someone became rebellious or couldn't pay off his loans, he was thrown out of the bank just like that. For every unpleasant situation, my father had his henchmen. We did not talk openly about such situations in our house. But I overheard it often enough, even though I spent most of my time at boarding school. Neither did we talk openly about my mother's addiction to pills and alcohol. This was an open secret. I was an only child, which neither of my parents would have expected. My father wanted to have two more boys to follow in his footsteps. The subject of having children lay over our family like a dark curse. My mother suffered one miscarriage after another. Either she lost her unborn children because of her addictions or the second assumption, the miscarriages first made her addicted to alcohol and tablets. Which came first, they didn't know? She always wanted to look slim, beautiful and socially acceptable. The pressures of having to look perfect, bearing children and being looked up to in luxury society were not always easy for her. When I was younger, I often heard my parents screaming and arguing in the middle of the night. This caused tons of dishes to break in the kitchen. My mother returned from a private doctor's office where the miscarriage was kept quiet. And at home she suppressed her tears in pills and more often in alcohol. And then, as so often, there were arguments. My father did not like miscarriages in his life and he did not have any sympathy for my mother. And then there was another problem. My mother thought that segregation was the invention of mankind. That's why she got particularly upset when a dark-skinned woman had the gall to work in our private doctor's office. My mother absolutely did not want this woman to see her exposed down below. The dark-skinned people were examined by my mother like insects. "Who does this woman think she is to see me naked down below? This woman has probably thrown herself ten times while I lie there and get the next scraping," my mother had so much hatred in her eyes as she uttered these sentences in a drunken stupor and in tears. I could watch it all from the stairs when I was home one weekend. She even tried to hit my father, but he rarely remained anti-aggressive in this case. He was holding my mother down and calming her down. Later, she slept off her frenzy in one of our many bedrooms. And I thought to myself that I never wanted to end up like that. I couldn't talk about these events to anyone, so I wrote them down in stories. I wrote it off my chest in metaphors, so to speak. But this was forbidden for me. Because I was the only descendant, my parents had great expectations of me that I could never fulfill; I was just not a boy.

1956

I was 16 years old and in the meantime I found friends at boarding school. With Sophia and Abigail I spent a great part of my life at the learning institution, which we sometimes called the marriage preparation school. We were given to jokes and all kinds of nonsense. We secretly tried alcohol on the boarding school grounds or hid from the professors and the supervisors in the toilet to smoke. We rebelled and felt really extraordinary. Sophia was the most fearless. She kept watch at the door and still managed to smoke a cigarette without being noticed. And she could drink like a fish. "We're just going to drink ourselves into this madhouse," she bellowed out. "Quiet! Sophia, if you keep yelling that loud, the bitch of a custodian will come and we'll get kicked out of school," Abigail got scared and I just stood there laughing, hoping no one heard us. I was finally on the same page with these two friends. They weren't as stuffy and obviously conformed as the other nerdy girls at this boarding school. We kept the fun and I remember back today that I rarely had such fun in my whole life as I did with Sophia and Abigail at that time. It wasn't until Mary that that feeling came back and lasted for many years.

I spent the summer with my parents in the Hamptons. This is where the high society of the United States of America met. While the ladies met to sip champagne and oysters, the gentlemen transacted new business. That's how the weeks in the Hamptons usually went. I usually sat at my window and watched my parents and the other guests of the luxury hotel patronize the dark-skinned servants. They were usually drivers or baggage handlers. For this I composed a story in which my father appeared as a dragon and my mother appeared in the form of the dragon's rolling tongue. In my imagination, the dragon was oversized and the porter, on the other hand, was very small. He tried to stab the dragon's rolling tongue with a pitchfork. But the dragon was bigger and stronger. It swallowed the man along with his pitchfork. I had to take good care that no one, but really no one would ever find this text. My parents would probably have locked me away forever. Lucky for me, I was always good at using hiding places for my own purposes.

My parents had another plan that summer that I didn't know about until later. They were obsessed with making a connection between me and Matthew Harris. His father dealt in diamonds and was one of the richest men in all of America. To my parents, this connection was hugely important; it would further enhance our public image. Matthew was the most sought-after bachelor there was in the rich man's market. Every girl was interested in him, except me. Which, of course, my parents noticed. It was a matter of time before he approached me. "You must be Ava. I've heard a lot about you," was his first flirty line to turn me on. "Good or bad?", I asked him. Like a suck-up, he came up and gave me a kiss on the hand. "Of course, only good. Or do you have some hidden skeletons in your closet?", Matthew appeared confident with me. That evening we went for a walk on the beach, which of course everyone could see. And for the benefit of my parents, they were constantly asked if anything was developing between him and me? "The two of them are made for each other. Ava is beauty and intelligence personified," my father flaunted at me. The parents of the other single, young ladies didn't like that at all. From there on, Matthew stuck to me like a tick I couldn't use. I disliked his manner. My mother did not miss the opportunity to point out to me how popular and desirable Matthew was, and that I should try harder to please him. My efforts could be improved, she criticized my lack of interest. Shortly before our departure there was a dinner including a ball. Everyone came in evening dress. I was also dressed up. I hated this display more and more the older I got. Matthew liked it, of course, when I stood before him like half an adult. "You look adorable," he whispered in my ear as I tried not to throw up. Then he handed me his pin. Which meant something like we belonged together. I hated everyone staring at me and talking about me. And I hated even more that arrangements were made about me without asking me. I could no longer stand my parents, Matthew, or the other guests. I even began to miss the strict boarding school. When the vacation was over, I went back to the boarding school in a bad mood and with a pin. There, word was already spreading that Matthew and

I had made acquaintances. This unwanted fact brought me even more envy and resentment from my comrades. Only Sophia and Abigail stood by me unconditionally. They even took pity on my person.

1957

Charming 17 years old I was and plunged into the world of future housewives. Our boarding school was not only there to inspire our intellectual abilities and make the most of us. As it seemed to me, it was a pretext to lure the girls out of their homes and pull money out of the fathers' pockets. In fact, first and foremost, and we quickly realized this, was to take courses that would prepare us to become the perfect wife, mother, and homemaker. The courses, ironically, we called preparation courses for creeping death. The single individual was to be traded for the mass-produced marriage. Trade books for hot plates, I didn't want to and couldn't make that deal that way. I had no intention of continuing to meet the slick Matthew Harris, let alone marry him. I wanted to study after school and fulfill myself. I'm sure I'll get married and have children, but certainly not with Matthew. Another woman should be happy to catch him. The nice thing about it was that Sophia and Abigail saw it the same way. That's why we hated the courses at boarding school. Literature, music, art, mathematics and philosophy; we liked those subjects. Chores, sewing, cooking, child rearing, and etiquette rules were pure torture for the three of us. Books like: The Perfect Hostess we unobtrusively avoided, while our classmates soaked that book up like chocolate. Olivia Preston, a classmate, complained to a teacher the other day why we needed to learn to iron when there were domestic servants? That was the thinking of most of us. I thought it was abhorrent to think that way. And everything I found disgusting I published under a pseudonym in the school newspaper. Everyone knew that the texts were written by me. However, my parents and the faculty were never allowed to know. Everyone kept quiet, even the girls who didn't like me. The little bit of solidarity was covered in this case and was not to be touched. On a rather muggy and warm Friday evening, it just so happened that Abigail, Sophia and I were not going home to our parents. And we knew that some professors were away on late summer vacation. Thus, there was also not enough supervisory staff at the boarding school, which they tried to conceal from us students. Sophia was always informed about everything and gave the green light for a forbidden Friday evening excursion. We freshened up and twisted the curlers in our hair. We pulled out the prettiest floral dresses from our dusty uniform closets, then set the scene with red lipstick. I had no idea where Sophia would take us? After sneaking out of the boarding school in all the darkness, a friend of Sophia's picked us up in his car. We had been driving for a long time to a fairly deserted area where I'm sure no one would know us. "Where are we?", I didn't know such areas. "In paradise," Sophia's good friend answered me. Abigail felt queasy. I, on the other hand, was attracted by the music coming from inside the building. The parking lot was bustling with activity. Many cars were parked here, which meant it would be crowded inside. When we walked in, we were looked at funny, but fully respected. Lots of people were milling around, it was hot and stuffy. I was fascinated by the music, the exuberant atmosphere and the people in here. Without a doubt, we had landed in a jazz bar. The waiter offered us the last free table. We three girlfriends had fun and visibly enjoyed the evening with a cold beer. My world consisted mainly of white people. In the jazz bar it was the other way around. Here was the world of dark-skinned people. I enjoyed observing this world where people danced and didn't have to carry the suitcases of white ladies. It was different and exciting, especially unfamiliar. But I felt comfortable. I liked this world. My friend Abigail was acting scared. She suspected that something terrible might happen to us. And that was only because of the fact that we were white. I could not share this fear and it proved to be completely unfounded. We sat on the bar stools and clapped to the rhythm of the music. I felt free, so incredibly free from any constraints. I was me, I was human. I noticed a dark-skinned man, also young, who shared a table with his friends near us. He was very handsome for my taste and looked friendly. He behaved quietly throughout the evening and what I found particularly great was that he was not drunk. It seemed to me that he was the same age as me. Unobtrusively I tried to observe him. I liked him right away. But apart from a glance on my part, nothing else had happened. The handsome, unknown man only looked over at me once, but that was it for the evening. The following Friday was another chance for us to sneak away. This was the last weekend before the regular school rush would start. Abigail, Sophia and I told our parents that we wanted to spend the weekend preparing and studying for the upcoming school year. That's why it was impossible for us to go home. Some of our teachers were invited to dinner this Friday night at a sponsor of the boarding school.

So our way led us to the jazz bar, where we already spent the last Friday evening. Abigail was more relaxed this time and let herself go. The whole evening I was desperately looking for the young man who had caught my eye last week. I was unlucky, contrary to my expectation, he wasn't there. His friends, on the other hand, were, which gave me hope that he would turn up at some point. Unfortunately this was not the case. And so we drove back to the strict boarding school at a late hour. "Aha. There you are again. There will be a reprimand and a lot of trouble for you. Prepare yourselves for a lot. And now remove that disgusting painting from your face. It's not good to look at. If your fathers didn't pay so much for your education, you could go back to where you came from. Now go wash your faces off!", the screaming of the supervisor could not be overheard. She brought another colleague as a witness, who stared at us as if we had been the last dirt. Caught off guard and in a gloomy mood, we retreated to our bedrooms after washing. We did not dare to talk anymore. The supervisor checked us until we were in bed. At some point this night, too, passed.

Soon after, I rode my bike to the print shop that was responsible for our internal school newspaper. Because we were organized girls, we financed the newspaper by means of non-taxed donations. And then someone said again, young women can't do money business. Oliver was our contact at the print shop. Every week he received the texts, which only had to be typeset correctly and sent to print. Most of the time, he met me at the entrance. The fact that he also printed our student paper between the serious daily newspaper was thanks to the additional three bottles of whisky that he received monthly from us authors. When I went back outside to unlock my bike, I spotted the interesting man I had once seen in the jazz bar. He was walking across the street with an older woman who was also dark-skinned. I thought to myself that this lady might be his mother? In his hands he held several shopping bags, which he kindly took from his companion. I just had to look at him and hoped that he would also take notice of me. My eyes did not leave him. And then it happened; he had also noticed me and looked across the street directly into my face. Shyly, we both then looked away again before our gazes met again. He continued walking down the street with the older lady and looked back at me once more. I was struck by lightning, so beautiful I found this man. Afterwards, I got on my bike and rode back to the boarding school, thinking of him every second. In my room, I told Sophia and Abigail that I saw the young man near the print shop and that our eyes met. Of course, I then wanted to go back to the jazz bar the next Friday. "Ava are you crazy? You can't do that. If they catch you, you'll be kicked out of boarding school. You know what that means. Your parents will freak out and either send you to a convent or marry you off as soon as they catch you. And you don't want that. Stay here and let it be!" Sophia recommended to me urgently and Abigail also nodded in agreement. I could hardly believe that she, of all people, was telling me this. Sophia was the wildest of the three of us. She had already tried everything that was dangerous and forbidden. Everyone knew her. She was notorious. And now she advised me to stay at the boarding school. But I could not. I couldn't get the man with the beautiful dark eyes out of my head. So the next Friday I sneaked out of the boarding school alone. Sophia's boyfriend took me to the jazz bar, but without staying. He was meeting another date and also warned me not to go to the bar alone as a white woman. I went in anyway. The curiosity about this man was too great. Like every Friday, the jazz dive was very crowded. I tried to find a place to sit down. I really wanted to see this attractive man again. To be honest, that was all I cared about. I would have liked to sink into the ground with nervousness. I liked the music very much, as well as the good mood of the people present. Suddenly my heart was beating like crazy, because there he was. The most attractive man I had ever seen. He sat down at the table with his friends and noticed me a short time later. It was strictly forbidden for me to be here, but there was nothing more beautiful right now. I smiled at him and he smiled back. Then he stood up and I thought he was coming to me. Instead, he went to the bar to get two drinks. I wanted to take the chance to get to know him. So I rose from my stool and walked straight toward him. He was already coming towards me with two soft drinks. "Hi. I'm Ava," I introduced myself. "Oh, hello Ava. My name is Jacob. Nice to meet you." We smiled up to each other's ears. Standing so close to me, I found him even more attractive than from a distance. We tried to talk, but it was too loud. Then we retreated to a quieter corner and talked for a while. I could have sat in that place with him all night. The time of day put a crimp in my plans, I should have been back at the boarding school by now. "Jacob, I'm sorry. It's getting late. I have to get back," I informed him. "Where do you have to go back to? I can take you home," that's the kind of reaction I expected from him. He was a good one. I could tell that right away. He knew how to drive and borrowed a friend's car. This time I really got scared. If the police caught a black man driving at night with a white woman in the passenger seat, they would both be in jail 100% of the time afterwards. That was too risky for me. I let him drive and hid in the back seat. Since I was slim, I could lie down easily without being noticed from the outside. Arriving at the boarding school, I thanked

Jacob. Then I quickly disappeared, because I didn't want to get caught again. That had just gone well and was a pure stroke of luck. None of the supervisors noticed me.

Saturday morning I was busy practicing for the classical concert. I played the cello. Since Sophia and Abigail were also in the concert, they had also come to practice and not gone home. At intermission, I ran up to the two of them, who could hardly wait to hear what I had to say. "It was glorious. And his eyes...", I gushed about Jacob and the girls listened intently. The next week we rehearsed without interruption for the important concert. All parents should see what outstanding abilities their daughters possessed on the instruments. My parents did not miss this event either. But not because they wanted to see me, but because it was a social event. Dressed in my boarding school uniform, I played the cello like a master. My parents would have had every reason to be proud of me. The crowd applauded, it was impossible not to hear. But nothing came from my parents. No praise or any other good word to me. I had not seen my mother or father for a long time. When we stood alone in the reception hall for a brief moment, my parents showed their true colors. "We have heard unpleasant news about you. You sneaked out of the boarding school without permission one Friday night and didn't return until night. That's what we've been told. And that you were out wearing makeup and a short dress. If you had done that at home, then ... and please stop writing this nonsense. We know that you run a school newspaper. Have you nothing but nonsense in your head? I'll have that beaten out of you. You're a disgrace, Ava. As soon as you graduate from high school, you're going to marry Matthew Harris. I hope he teaches you more sense," my father said to me in a serious tone. I felt like I was sitting in the dock. "I don't want to marry him!" I rebelled. "Yes you will Miss, and until then you will keep quiet. Is that clear?" my mother could kill with her looks. I ran crying to the bathroom and hid there until the commotion was over. My parents drove home after the event without giving me a kind or benevolent word. I went to bed, not wanting to live like this. I lay in my bed with my eyes open and couldn't fall asleep. Until suddenly there was a knock on my window. I got a shock because my room was further up in the apartment building. Who should be able to knock on my window? I pushed the curtains to the side and actually saw Jacob before my eyes. Pleased, but also irritated, I reacted to the reunion. "Hello, beautiful Ava. How are you?" he had actually climbed up the tree outside my window and was sitting on a branch. I felt like I was in Romeo and Juliet. "How? I mean, how did you know which window to knock on? And how did you sneak onto the premises?", I wanted to know, and at the same time I was most impressed with his dedication. He had never told me how he knew where my room was and how to get there. He also always concealed from me how he got to the guarded compound without attracting attention. "A true gentleman enjoys and keeps quiet," was all he had to say about it. I felt a tingle in my stomach, it felt magical. A moment that was never to end. We looked deep into each other's eyes, then he gently and lovingly stroked my face. "You are so beautiful," he said to me. To me, he was, too. And even though I didn't know him well at all, I would have rather married him than Matthew Harris. Out of pure affection for each other, we kissed for the first time. It felt more beautiful than anything I'd ever felt. "You better go before you get caught and locked up," I regretfully had to tell him. We kissed goodbye one more time before he jumped down from the tree. He ran off and I looked after him until I couldn't see anything. Only then did I close my window and lay down in bed. Full of happy hormones, I still couldn't fall asleep. But it didn't matter. I had finally seen Jacob and gotten a kiss from him. At some point I fell asleep and began to dream sweetly.

From then on we began to meet secretly. He left an address with me at the boarding school, which was given to me through an intermediary. I should come to the given address. Initially, a flirt between me and Jacob developed, which was to become more. Of course, my girlfriends got to know that I went to him in every free minute. In the first time they said nothing to it, because they knew that I liked Jacob in some way very much. Our time at boarding school left little opportunity for free time. The days were planned through with education from morning to night. Everything here was organized and structured down to the smallest detail. In addition to the usual classes, there were marriage preparation classes, music lessons, and project work. We held debates and lectures, took up scientific and political work. On us were bred the women of tomorrow. An educated American woman should, of course, do something for her figure. So there were various lessons in which we had to be physically active: gymnastics, swimming, horseback riding, playing tennis or golf. We were taught all this. Thus, my days were usually structured and there was hardly any private time left for me besides studying. Besides, I was about to graduate from high school. I had to compromise to be able to see Jacob. I covered up my leaving the boarding school with the excuse of going to the print shop. It was known that we young women published an internal and closed student newspaper among ourselves. Therefore, they let me go without any fuss. The second excuse came to mind. I would have to do research for the newspaper. Because this is a journalistic activity that needed to be learned, I was not stopped from doing it either. So I used the excuses to my advantage and drove out to the country to visit Jacob whenever I could. He worked as a carpenter; this was not only his profession, but also his passion. First, he showed me around the carpentry shop. I was visibly impressed by what he used to make out of wood. He was gifted and possessed great talent. That is why he approached his work with enthusiasm every day. I had fallen in love not only with Jacob, but also with his carvings. What he created with his hands was almost unimaginable to me. Everyone has been given a talent, a special gift. And Jacob's gift was to work in the workshop and make beautiful things out of wood with his hands. I felt very comfortable with him and in the carpentry shop where we always met. There were two worlds in which I lived. One world could not have been richer in money. There was upbringing and education built on the wealth of the parents. But people kept to themselves. Elite was associated with elite. Dark-skinned people remained only unskilled workers and servants. The other world was Jacob for me. He was poor and yet he radiated a happiness I had never seen before. Over time, great affection developed between us and affection became serious love. A love like I had never experienced before. Apart from Sophia and Abigail, he was the only one who knew me as I really was. Of course, not everyone liked our connection. Outside of the carpentry shop, we were constantly looked at with disdain. The stares hit us and we knew exactly why we were being gazed at, like people in the circus. It was our skin color, which could not have been more different. I was a white young woman, he was a black young man. We didn't have a problem with it, but many of our peers did. At first, our friends didn't say much about the friendship. Eventually, they turned away from us. They didn't stick with us anymore. "Ava, you know how dangerous this love affair is. Do you want to risk your life for this man? Surely Jacob is nice, much nicer than Matthew. But if this gets out, you're dead!", Sophia was able to phrase badass. There was no embellishing the situation with her. Abigail nodded again in agreement. From then on, we were on our own. None of our friends stuck by us anymore. Our relationship had become all the stronger for it. Jacob stood by me and I by him. Our relationship with each other was based on respectful interaction. He was kind to me and made me laugh all the time. We did each other good and I could learn a lot from him. Humanity, helpfulness and trust were not something I was born with. Jacob, on the other hand, I could trust, more and more every day.

1958

One day I stayed in the carpenter's shop until evening. I didn't want to go back to boarding school yet. It was too nice to be with the man I loved. He gave me warmth and security, which I had always missed before. It was getting dark and the stars were shining in the sky. By now we were the only people in the carpenter shop. The other men had already gone home. There was a barn behind the carpentry shop. Maybe it was the moon that took us there. I don't remember. Hand in hand we stood in the barn and kissed intimately. His hands touched me. It felt good and right. While the stars shone brightly in the sky, in that place I experienced the greatest passion and love I ever dared to dream of. We discovered love, we made love. Not for a second of my life did I regret this happiness. We were connected to the elements of this earth. The sky was over us like a protective blanket. Arm in arm, we lay in the barn afterwards, silently enjoying the moment. As beautiful as the evening was, I had to return to the boarding school. I would have loved to spend the whole night with him, if possible even forever. But I could not and was not allowed to. Jacob took me back in his uncle's car to the place that was so different from where I had stayed before. Our farewell kiss was still romantic, then I dashed rationally realistic back to the boarding school. I had previously bribed the guard at the entrance with a pack of cigarettes so that he would let me in later without fuss. Fortunately, I succeeded. I heard some professors talking in the library, so I tiptoed quietly past them. Thank heavens, I holed up in my room without attracting attention. I felt like an agent leading a double life. Exciting, but also dangerous.

A short time later, I successfully graduated from high school. Only Jacob's and my luck were not to last forever. The night in the barn was not without consequences for us. My periods stopped and I often felt nauseous in the morning. I was pregnant. Had just graduated from college and was still a tender 18 years old. When I told Jacob the news, his eyes smiled with joy. He took me in his arms, showing me that he stood by me and the child. Neither of us knew what to do next? Therefore, in our inexperienced way, we let it come to us. My parents pushed me to marry Matthew Harris against my will. Early in the morning, my mother had me picked up to take me to the most exclusive bridal store in all of Mississippi. I fought it tooth and nail and made a fuss, but it didn't help. The most expensive dress was, of course, meant for me. While the saleswoman was lacing the corset of the dress tighter and tighter and I could hardly breathe, my mother was already sitting drunk on an armchair at ten o'clock in the morning with a glass of champagne in her hand, watching me get worse and worse. I finally had to throw up. The saleswoman looked at my mother in shame as the precious dress became the victim of my vomit. "Is it the excitement or are you missing something?" my mother asked me in the tone of a commanding officer. I actually dared to vomit all over the most expensive dress. My mother would have loved to drag me out of the store by my hair, but she was already too tipsy for that. She didn't lose her instinct despite the alcohol and she put one and one together. "Wait a minute. You refuse to marry the most popular bachelor in the whole South and then you throw up in the morning. Ava, you're not pregnant, are you?" My silence gave her the answer. The anger on her face was worse than any prison they would put me in. We drove to my parents' house. There I was locked in my room until my father came home from the bank in the evening. The next day they had me examined by their private physician and good family friend, Doctor Houston Senior. He immediately confirmed my pregnancy, which for my parents was the biggest disaster of their lives so far. They didn't even ask who the child was from? They didn't care. "The abortion is next week. Until then, you stay in your room!" my mother threw the horrible information at my head. I couldn't believe what I was hearing. Abortion? Me? Anything but that! I would rather have killed myself than allow my unborn child to be killed. Just like at the boarding school, there was a tall tree in front of my room window at home. This gave me the idea to climb up the tree through my window. From there to somehow carefully get down to the ground. I was athletic and dared to do it. Besides, I had seen Jacob do it before. My father was at work and my mother was teasing the maids. She noticed late that I was no longer in my room. I ran away, my destination was to lead me to Jacob. He welcomed me with open arms and gave me everything I needed. I felt cared for and loved. During the day, I spent time with him in the carpentry shop or with his family. In the evenings we had dinner together with his family. They lived in poor conditions, yet with faith in God and the miracle of a positive outlook on life. I was welcome there. Nevertheless, Jacob and I were very afraid that at any moment the police might tear us apart. His family liked me very much, but I could tell that they were also afraid of the consequences of our love affair. Jacob fed me and created a feeling of love and care during the difficult time between us. I was so grateful to him. He tried not to let his fear show. I, on the other hand, could not hide it so well. Despite the fear, I stayed with him in poverty. There could have been an easier way for me, but I didn't want that. The only thing I wanted was Jacob and our child. My parents, of course, immediately informed the police. With a large search party, they quickly found what they were looking for. Someone told them where I was at that time. When the police car drove in our direction, Jacob and I hid in the carpenter's shop. I had never been so afraid for my future. I could not and would not imagine a life without Jacob. The policemen showed up at our house with several of them. They tore us apart as if we were wild animals. Jacob wanted to protect and hold me and the unborn baby, but we were no match for the cops. They brutally pulled me into the patrol car and then drove to the police station. From the back seat, I watched my loved one go. At the station, they put me in a barren cell. Jacob got it worse. Three policemen beat him to a pulp. His friends and family had to watch. They would have been shot if they had helped him. In his own blood, he lay there unable to move. I was released from jail the next day on bail by my parents and taken from there to the next jail, my own home. My belly had grown so it had been too late for an abortion. I remained in my room in the dark about what had happened to Jacob. I would have liked nothing more than to hear a sign of life from him.

1959

I was 19 years old and thus not yet of age in the USA. Thus, my parents still retained the greatest power over me and my life. I was not allowed to make my own decisions until two years later. That did not benefit me in this case. Glad that it had been too late for an abortion, yet devastated to have been caught in my parents' clutches. I had to spend the rest of the pregnancy alone in my room without any contact with the outside world. Of course, I was also forbidden to have any contact with the father of my unborn child. Unfortunately, he could not get close to me either. What Jacob and I had done was forbidden by the police in Mississippi. In fact, strictly forbidden. Our love affair and the result it produced could mean death for both of us. My parents were not interested in me or the child in my womb. They were completely indifferent to how I was doing. When I went into labor, I was alone in my room. Only when I began to scream loudly did my mother enter my room in disgust. Shielded, they took me to the office of our private physician, Dr. Houston Senior. He was not only our doctor, but also a family friend. My parents knew him well and vice versa. In the greatest pain of labor, I lay there and secretly had my first and only child. A beautiful, enchanting daughter. I could not have imagined the looks on my parents' faces any worse. Perhaps they still secretly hoped that I would give birth to a child with white skin. But the fact was that the man I loved was a colored man. And with that, just like Jacob, our child was blessed with a dark skin color. Doctor Houston and a colored midwife helped me give birth. My parents were incensed that our friend and doctor provided a colored midwife for me. And they were even more incensed because my child did not meet their expectations. I beamed with happiness at the sight of my daughter. She was the most beautiful thing I had ever seen in 19 years. But I missed Jacob immensely. He most likely would have burst into tears at the birth. When the birth was over, my parents were quick to go about business as usual. No one took any notice of me. As quickly as we had come unnoticed, we disappeared again in the night and fog. At home I was again locked in my room, only this time not alone. They left my daughter with me. I was still weak and bleeding. It had been less than three hours since the birth. My child felt comfortable in my arms and she felt my excessive love. I had to cry because I was so touched by the face of my daughter. It took a while until she opened her eyes. When they finally opened, her eyes shone and sparkled like diamonds in the morning light. And I enjoyed the time she was in my arms. I didn't realize what was going to happen? That's why I drew strength and memory from every moment I spent with her. The midwife from the doctor's office knew Jacob's family, so she kept him informed. He knew that his daughter and I were locked in my parents' house. It came to the most beautiful moment of my whole life. In the middle of the night, Jacob had entered our compound and climbed up the tree in front of my window. He threw a rock against the window pane. I sensed immediately that it was him. I don't remember exactly how he did it, but he jumped from the thick branch right into my room. I would have loved to rejoice with joy, but we kept quiet. The danger was too great that my parents would notice us and destroy our only moment as a family. We kissed in greeting, as if we hadn't seen each other in years. Jacob took my hand and walked with me step by step to the bed where our daughter lay. She must have been a feast for his eyes. Jacob's eyes filled with boundless love. He wept with happiness. The appearance of our daughter was the culmination of our love for each other. "Hello. Welcome to the world my little daughter," he took her in his arms and still could hardly believe it. "How have you been? And how was the birth? Ava, I'm so truly sorry I wasn't there. I wanted to be so much. But the main thing is that you're both doing well. As soon as you're well, I'll take you both to my place. We'll make it!", Jacob gave me hope and I believed every word he said. He really wanted to live with me and our daughter together. At that moment I knew that I loved the right man. He already risked so much for me, which not every man would accomplish in such a situation. We whispered the whole time. There was never such a happy moment for me again. Jacob kissed me, held my hand, and stroked my back. We were both immensely proud to have created something so great. He held our baby in his arms full of care, as if she were the most beautiful rose in the whole wide world. "Annabelle?" he asked me. "Yes, Annabelle," I answered without hesitation. Our daughter's name was frankly perfect for both of us. Jacob looked lovingly into my eyes, then pulled out something. "What do you have there?", I whispered to him curiously and questioningly. "My Ava. It's a gift for both of you. A heart that I carved myself. When you pull it apart, it creates two halves. One half is to be for you and the other half is for our daughter Annabelle. And when you put the two halves back together, you make a whole heart. You two are my heart; forever and ever," Jacob handed me one half and placed the other half next to our offspring. Annabelle knew we were her parents. I was so touched by the personal gift that Jacob would forever own my heart beating inside me. "I'll get you guys to me as soon as I can as well. See you soon. I love you," Jacob kissed me and Annabelle goodbye. Then he disappeared through my window, jumped up the tree and disappeared into the night.

It was the last time I saw him alive.

He was treacherously shot the next day by two white men. His blood was spread all over the carpentry shop in the place where he carved the heart for me and our daughter at that time. Here his own heart beat for the very last time. When I learned of his death, I broke down. I didn't want to live anymore myself, but I had to go on for our daughter Annabelle. When she would grow up, I wanted to tell her all about her father and that he was a good man. The gardener who tended our property sent me the message informing me of Jacob's parents' death. I don't know who were the two white men who killed him in the back? Anyway, they were never found and charged. To me, this was no coincidence. Jacob was a kind and respectful person. He didn't run up debts, never did anything malicious to anyone. The only thing he did was to love me. And I was convinced that that was why he had to pay with his life. Apparently, the right to life for everyone did not apply to us. His daughter was deprived of the chance to ever know him with his death. His family and friends were never able to speak to him or see him again. The pain of losing the man I loved more than anything was almost unbearable for me. My world, my hopes and wishes were shattered with his death. Inwardly I was destroyed.

It was to get worse. My parents made a significant decision that was to change my entire life in a lasting and far-reaching way. However, in the worst possible way. The next morning, my mother came storming into my room without notice. Her hatred against me and my child knew no bounds. She tore my sleeping daughter out of my arms. Annabelle woke up and started screaming loudly. "Give me back my child!", I begged my mother. She did not respond to my words and went towards the door. I was faster, in no time I was able to hold the door shut. "What are you doing? Where are you taking my daughter? She belongs to me. Give her back to me right now!", I yelled at my mother. Uncertainty, fear and panic spread through me. Whatever was going to happen, I couldn't let it happen. But she continued to remain as cold as a block of ice. My father stood at the door from the outside and pushed it open firmly. I was pushed aside and my mother was able to escape with Annabelle. I did not give up, resisted and fought unwaveringly. Screaming, I ran down the stairs and after my mother as fast as I could. There was a car in the driveway from which an old lady got out. My parents greeted the woman, who then quickly received Annabelle. The maids were ordered in advance by my parents to hold me. I could not reach my child. The old lady got into the car together with my daughter and they were driven away. The strange woman did not turn around, she did not look over at us again. She ignored my shouting apathetically. She seemed as cold and heartless as my parents. "Who is this woman? And what is she doing with my child? Get Annabelle back for me. Get her back!", I was beside myself. My scream should have been heard all over Mississippi. I kicked around and was half on the floor. I couldn't give up my daughter without a fight. To my parents, this was just a treatise of things to do. It was a formal thing for them, not an emotional one. My father and mother simply informed me that I would never see my daughter again. The old lady from earlier would have been responsible for placing my child in foster care. There my daughter would stay forever and be adopted by the family. That was all. My parents disappeared without expressing even the slightest sympathy for me. My father did his work in the bank and my mother went to the city social gathering of highly respected ladies. And I, I stayed behind. Never before had I felt such sorrow and pain. I had lost everything, the love of my life and our common daughter. The two people I loved should not be allowed to stay in my life. My parents took everything that was dear to me. I wanted to die, my life no longer made sense without Jacob and Annabelle. My parents had me taken to my room, the door was locked several times. Immediately I took one half of the carved heart. It had fallen to the floor in the heat of the moment. Then I searched my whole room for the second half, to my disappointment I found nothing. I seriously wondered if my parents gave the old lady the heart for Annabelle? And how would they know about it? I could not imagine that, but at least let it never be found again. I cried for several days and thought about suicide.

After a long, endless, desperate mourning, I left my parents' house to study literature. As far away from home as possible. My parents, meanwhile, canceled their arranged marriage to the exceedingly wealthy Matthew Harris, which initially damaged their upper-class reputation. They invented a plausible excuse to appease the Harris family and to continue to make their mark on them. There was a rift between me and my parents. I did not want to and could not see them anymore. They had caused me too much pain and had never accepted me for who I really was. My written articles and stories, Jacob and Annabelle were swept under the rug by them. I never saw my parents again. It was said about my mother that she died one day from her addiction to alcohol and pills. My father, they said, thereafter indulged in his various mistresses and increased his fortune annually through harsh methods.

I, on the other hand, never again loved a man the way I once loved Jacob. Infinitely and daily I missed him and Annabelle. With Jacob, it was clear to me that he would never come back. He had died and this fact could not be undone. Our daughter Annabelle was still alive. That was the difference. I didn't know where and with whom? When I graduated with a high degree in literature, I was determined to have my daughter with me. There was nothing more important to me. For years I thought about her day and night. My heart was broken and the pain was still as if she had been taken away from me yesterday. I looked for her everywhere and got information. Every agency that was responsible for families and adoptions got a visit from me. But no one could or would give me any information about my daughter.

Then I began to write. I became a writer by profession and even unexpectedly successful. I have written 50 novels about love so far. Writing romance novels reminded me of the love of my life, Jacob. I had lost him, but the love he gave me then remained unforgotten for me. And why there was not a single child in my novels was because my only child was given away against my will. This pain is still deep and firm in me today. The attempt to have a child appear as a character in my 51st novel has failed so far. I felt inhibited and blocked. The novel was never finished.

That was my story ...

21.

Back at the Louisiana hospital

Ava was still sitting in the hospital bed next to Annabelle as she finished telling her personal story. Everyone present was moved and in tears from the events they heard from the old life-experienced lady. She gave a detailed account of her entire life from Mississippi. Isabella, Benjamin and Thomas sat around the two hospital beds. Even Benji, who had known Ava well for years, was unaware of the octogenarian's fateful history. He was so touched by Ava's experiences in earlier years that he now understood her. Now he knew why the writer never mentioned a child in her novels. "What a story," Isabella was visibly moved. Annabelle and Ava looked at each other differently after this news than before. Ava found her missing daughter after 60 years. And Annabelle finally found her mother. Both women found themselves together again after such a long time of longing hope. In tears, they both rose from their hospital beds and embraced; tentatively at first, then intimately. Thomas, Isabella and Benjamin applauded. The family was finally united. Both ladies embraced, placed their hand on each other's face, and could not take their eyes off each other. Ava gave her sixty-year-old daughter a kiss on the forehead. "Now I've finally found you. And after such a long time. I never thought I would live to see this. And now you're here. You're standing in front of me in the flesh, Annabelle," Ava was moved and overwhelmed by her feelings. She knew that only Jacob's heart brought her and her daughter back together. That was his gift. He fulfilled his final task from above and thus reunited the love of his life with his daughter together at last. Isabella also finally found what she had been searching for so long. The needle in the haystack actually existed. She brought her grandmother into her life. Isa stood crying in her father's arms. For a brief moment, the twenty-year-old paused. Her heart was missing someone all the time. And suddenly, that feeling of longing was no longer there. Ava was her grandmother. Fate, chance, or destiny, whatever it was, brought them together in this life. "I checked it off for myself because the subject was weighing too heavily on my mind. The longing for you was great and I also never thought you would ever be in front of me. I am 60 years old today," Annabelle shared out of occasion and need. "It was pure luck that I was placed in a loving foster family shortly after my birth. Many children who shared the same fate as me often changed families. I, on the other hand, was adopted by my foster parents. I grew up there and could not have asked for a better foster family. From the beginning, they were there for me. They were by my side and stuck by me even when things got rough. And yet I kept my half of the heart I had carved myself with me at all times. I carried it with me so that on one side I knew my adoptive parents were with me and on the other side I knew the heart of my birth family.

I never knew what this wooden heart meant? And from whom I got it or who owns the other half? But I always felt that I was still loved by someone out there. This knowledge brought me strength. It was always there, it had been given to me when I came to my foster parents. It was the only thing I was given from home. At school, I was always at the top of my class, a little nerd, so to speak. And I think, Isabella, that you want to do good is something you inherited from me. After school, I studied social pedagogy with the intention of helping poor and dark-skinned people. And that's what I've been doing professionally all my life. And I love to do good deeds. Of course, in recent years I have reduced my working hours, I would never have wanted to do it any other way," Isabella and Thomas looked at Annabelle with gratitude. They knew that Annabelle was extremely cut back professionally. Chronic heart muscle inflammation and her daughter's associated hospitalizations made it no longer possible to work full time. Isabella gradually realized how much her mother was giving up for her. Isa embraced both her mother and her grandmother. The three of them together made a beautiful picture. Annabelle continued, "I have the best man by my side that there could be for me. Even though I am constantly worried about his job, I thank God every day that I have him with me. I got used to worrying all the time. My daughter was seriously ill and my husband works as a police officer. That makes you appreciate more the things you have right now. Because I never met my real mother, I didn't want a child of my own at first. But Thomas was the right one for me. That's why I decided to become a mother after all and had my only daughter Isabella relatively late, at the age of 40. My little family turned out to be the greatest happiness for me. I got the information that my father was a dark-skinned man who unfortunately had died at an early age. And I possessed the news that my mother was a light-skinned woman. Other than that, I knew nothing at all about my parents and their situation. For a while I tried with all my willpower to find out more knowledge about my biological parents, but I was not successful. My husband supported me in the search even he as a policeman and we both together, found out nothing. No one could give us any information. Everywhere I left my address and phone number with the request to contact me if there was ever any news in my case. No one ever got back to me. There was only one thing left for me to do. I had to accept the situation as it was. And I did. I could handle it. But in the back of my mind there was always the longing to know where I came from? Today I received a gift. My mother Ava. And I thank my daughter Isabella for her persistence in finding her biological grandmother."

Overflowing with tears, mother and daughter embraced each other again. Thomas and Benjamin also gave free rein to their feelings. And Isabella? She felt as if she had just experienced a birthday and Christmas together. Ava's health was better, she no longer needed to stay in the hospital as a patient.

Annabelle was also discharged from the same hospital. Together they all went to the home of Annabelle and her family. Ava spent a few beautiful days with her family. She enjoyed every hour with her daughter Annabelle and her granddaughter Isabella. Benjamin, of course, had also stayed. He somehow belonged to Ava and was the new friend at Isabella's side. Thus, he was a part and complete member of this family. For Ava and Annabelle, the gift of time together was like a colorful dream. They talked a lot about each other and tried to make up for the lost time as best they could. Even though they knew that this was not possible. They knew that time is a precious commodity. Time is finite. Ava was already 80 years old and her daughter Annabelle 60. Neither could guess how many moments they had left together? Their time together was their dearest gift. After a few wonderful days, Ava and Benjamin traveled back to Mississippi. Ava, of course, got back her half of the heart that Isabella had secretly borrowed from her earlier. The heart finally brought the family together. "Thank you to my grandfather Jacob, up there in heaven. I salute you," Isabella called upward, looking toward the horizon. She also greeted Mary up there in heaven. For Mary lent Isabella her heart and thus led her to Ava. And Jacob's heart ultimately led Ava to Annabelle.

The family wanted to see each other again soon and never lose each other again.

22.

Ava and Benji, meanwhile, had arrived back home in Mississippi. Benjamin described the incredible news from Louisiana to his parents. There were two things for the parents to process. First, their son and Isabella were now lovers. The Isabella who received the heart of his late Aunt Mary. And second, and this was probably the biggest news for Benjamin's parents, Ava was the missing grandmother of that same Isabella. Stunned, Benji's mother and father received the news. "Then I guess your Isabella is really part of our family now," Benjamin's father rejoiced. His mother, who was initially critical of Isabella, looked on the relationship with the twenty-year-old with favor. "Someone up there apparently wanted our family and her family to get together. And with that, we're also connected to Ava for eternity. I'm sure your aunt would have liked that," Benjamin's mum spoke to her son. "She's a good girl and if her parents are just as good people, we'll call them welcome to our Mississippi home," his father added. "Yes, they are very good people. You will like them," Benji gushed about his steady girlfriend's parents.

Meanwhile, another person was completely absorbed and busy. Ava holed up in her writing room to finish the 51st novel. But she destroyed her previous manuscript down to the last page and started writing all over again. And this time, not a typical Ava romance novel, but something unusual for her. Remembering Jacob, her unique love, her daughter and her life so far, she found the strength, courage and fortitude to put this story into words. Ava wrote her authentic story, this time not conventionally worded. She now knew what she had to write. From the first page to the last, she retreated to her office and didn't stop until her story was written. In it, she told the story of her life and love. The story about the three of them who were supposed to be together forever. The story about Ava, Jacob and Annabelle. She brought back to her mind all the memories from that time and wrote them down. It felt like she was just reliving it herself. She was reliving every situation. The memories came to life. Her story and her love were not hidden from now on. Everyone should be able to read what one of the most famous female writers in the USA used to experience personally. Every reader possessed an image, a conception of the writer Ava in her head. "The educated, white, old lady. She has become very rich through her novels. She must be doing well with that," is what most of her readers thought about her. None of her followers knew what her fate was in the past. So she wrote until the last page until the end. She formulated notes and memories with a pen on paper. Ava typed the autobiographical summary of her personal history on her old typewriter. This was to have been her final work. When she was finished, she pushed the typewriter aside and took a very deep, firm breath. She sat back and grew tired.

A few hours later in Louisiana

At Annabelle's home, the phone rang. The sixty-year-old answered it and became very quiet. She hardly said a word, and it seemed as if she had just received no joyful news. Thomas approached his wife and asked her what had happened? Full of grief, she fell into his arms. "How are we going to explain this to Isabella?", Annabelle looked at her husband questioningly. The usually articulate policeman was clueless himself in this case. "I don't know. Honey, I just don't know. I'm unspeakably sorry for both of you," he tried to find the right words. The two went upstairs and had something to tell their daughter. They hadn't wanted to do that so soon. They knocked on Isabella's room door and then entered. Without saying a word, they looked at their daughter and hugged her tightly. Isabella immediately sensed that something was wrong. And so it was.

It was Ava's death, which her parents announced in mourning.

"This can't be happening. We still had so much planned for her. Christmas we were going to spend together," now Isabella searched for her grandmother for a long time; then finally found her and lost her again. "Honey, I know. It hurts immensely. But maybe it was just the right time for her to go? A lot has happened to her. Good and bad. And everything that needed to be taken care of had been accomplished. She had found me as her daughter. And you as her grandchild, Isabella. Then she got the chance to tell us her whole story. Now I know why I was adopted and who my father was. Benjamin's mother just told me on the phone that Ava had been doing very well the last few weeks. She was happy and seemed very content. Then everything in her life must have been right, she had done everything and experienced everything. Her personal circle was closed, nothing remained open or unfulfilled. Apparently she chose that moment for herself to leave our earth," Annabelle found fitting words to describe her mother who had just met her. Isabella could understand the reasoning, but was still sad not to be able to see her grandmother in the flesh.

The very next day, Benjamin was at Isabella's door. He rode the Greyhound bus from Mississippi all night to Louisiana. Surprised and overjoyed, the young man was met by Isa and her parents. Katy was also visiting with Isabella. She introduced the two of them to each other. Her best friend was immediately pleased with her new friend's choice. "At your wedding, I want to be the first bridesmaid," Katy announced joyfully in advance. The three had to laugh. "Who knows what the future holds? But I know one thing for sure. You are a part of my future," Benjamin's message went to his Isabella. The two took each other by the hand and knew they were meant for each other. The very next day, the smitten Benji made a proposal to Isabella's parents, "After

Ava's funeral in Mississippi, I would consider moving in with her family in Louisiana. I would like to be serious about being with their daughter. That is, of course, if they are okay with it?" Isabella knew nothing of all this, but could hardly hide her excitement. What would her parents say to that? "Well, first of all, you don't have to say you. You're allowed to call us by our first names. And then my wife and I think you'd be a good fit for our daughter. That's why you're welcome to move in with us in a few weeks," Thomas confirmed, also on behalf of his wife. Isabella and Benjamin kissed each other with joy, expressing their affection for each other.

But first, the funeral of their beloved Ava was to take place in Mississippi.

The Epilogue

Today in Mississippi, USA

Meanwhile, night has fallen. I told our story from beginning to end. All the mourners have stayed to listen to our shared story to the end. My parents are both sitting next to me holding my hand. Benji sits on the back of the couch behind me and holds his hand protectively on my shoulder. In the meantime, it has become quiet in the living room. The mourners present are crying and passing tissues to each other. "So, we've never heard anything like this before," the awakened neighbors give as feedback to me. "There we were, knowing Ava for so long and yet knowing nothing about her," others say. "Sad. Just sad," mentions a woman from the helpful charity.

We say goodbye to the mourners at Ava's front door. Everyone shakes our hands. "Glad you guys got together after all," one says. "Thank you for telling us everything so openly. I would never have guessed about this fate," says the woman with the curly mane on her head. We are shown a lot of sympathy, love and gratitude. Of course, we also notice great sadness for a great woman. My grandmother Ava.

My parents, Benjamin, his parents and I clean up the house together. We put the used dishes in Ava's kitchen, which seems so lifeless without her and Mary. We want to leave everything clean and tidy. But we can't sleep in Ava's house at this point. Not at all right after the funeral. Benjamin's parents invite us to spend the night with them. We gratefully accept the offer after Ava's house is shining again.

The next day, we visit the grave of our sorely missed Ava once again. We want to give her one last gift on the way. My mom and I put the two halves of the heart that her great love Jacob once carved for her and my mom into Ava's grave. We place both halves as one whole on the casket. My dad and Benji, along with the pastor of the church, now fill the grave with dirt. So goes my grandmother Ava and with her the heart that brought us all together and reunited us. Together we leave the cemetery with the best memories of her life. I know that one day I will see her again. But until then, I have a great life waiting for me to experience. And when the time comes one day, I'll be ready to look her in the eye again to tell her how much I love her.

Two months later

Benjamin inherits my grandmother Ava's house out of the blue. She has always felt how much it means to him to be able to visit her and Mary. Benji learned a lot from the two women together in the past and from each of their own. This house kept him from going off the rails. Ava created a place of peace, security and togetherness with this building. That's probably why she bequeathed it to Benjamin. She knew he would appreciate this place. Benji was blindsided when he received the news of the inheritance. So the plan to move to Louisiana with me is no more.

What we did with the house and our love?

Time passes and I turn 23 this year. Accordingly, I have been of age in the United States of America for a long time. When Benjamin suggested that I move to Mississippi to live with him, I didn't have to think for three seconds. We belong together and my heart is finally beating in time. I have found what I was looking for so long. We have made Ava's house a place for everyone. Together we run and manage the house in memory of Jacob, Ava and Mary. They would be visibly proud of what we have created. In the place for everyone, there is daily singing, talking and creating a peaceful gathering. Writing classes are offered for the illiterate. We affectionately call the writing courses the Ava courses. In addition, the charity to which Ava and Mary belonged has its new headquarters here. I moved to Mississippi completely and couldn't imagine anything better for my life. My mom was still saying the other day, "It came as it was meant to come. It was meant to be that you do something good for other people."

And in the evening, when I sit on your porch, I look up at the twinkling stars. Benjamin sits next to me and holds my hand. My life couldn't be more beautiful. Who would have thought it, after my long illness, endless search and loss? I realize that you often have to go through a dark time to one day feel light in your heart again. And I feel my light is you. My heart is you. You are with me and in me. You are in every twinkling star, in every ray of sunshine, and in every shining flower of your garden. You live on in your stories and in our hearts. I am a part of your story and your story is a part of me. Your two hearts in heaven brought us together. Mary, by lending me her heart, and through it I came to know you. Jacob by carving the two halves of the heart that reunited my mother and you.

I carry your best friend's heart inside me as if it were my own. Even though Mary only lent it to me, I take care of it as if it were my most precious gift.

But my heartbeat comes from you alone. You are the drive of the beat that makes my heart beat in perfect love. You are forever, you are me. Your love for Jacob, lives on in me through my love for Benjamin.

My heart, it beats for you.

End.

Each of us carries a heart within us.

Use your heart peacefully.

Use peace for the benefit of man, for animals, for nature, for our earth.

If you walk in peace, you walk with your heart.

If you go with your heart, peace will reign and love will follow in every place you leave behind.

Source Notes:

Cover design: Stephanie Doench, 2023

Longing (poem), Doench, Stephanie, 2021: page 119.